XANDER'S MATE

THE QUINTON SHIFTERS SERIES

ABIGAIL RAINES

CONTENTS

CHAPTER ONE: XANDER

"Xander?"

I jerk awake, confused for just a second. The backseat of this particular car is obviously far too comfortable. I fell asleep long enough to dream of wolves, wolves from all over the world...fighting each other. I have dark dreams from time to time and I can usually resolve not to think of them too much. This one disturbed me a little bit. I dreamed of wolves going at each other as they would go at the greatest of enemies. Perhaps it was just another bit of aftermath from the Hardwidge debacle. It's been a long time, but I still think of that night that I, Mason and Aaron freed Micah from that awful pack of monsters.

"Yes, Betsy," I say sighing. I roll my shoulder and see my driver glance at me in the rear-view mirror. Betsy has been with me a few years now. She's a bear shifter from Kansas. I like to have the people working closest to me in such positions be shifters whenever possible. Nobody wants to have to hide who they are every moment of the day. "I'm awake."

"Can't burn the candle at both ends," Betsy says cheerfully, as she pulls into the parking structure behind the Tremblay Company headquarters outside Quinton.

"Sure you can," I say, rubbing my eyes. "You're just likely to burn your fingers."

"What's too much today?" Betsy says drily. "The alpha thing or the CEO thing? Or just being a Tremblay in general?"

I bristle at that. Juggling my duties as alpha to the most powerful family in my clan with my job as CEO of The Tremblay Company *can* be exhausting but I can certainly handle it.

I have to. It's what has always been expected of me.

"It's never too much," I say, snapping just a little.

"Of course not," Betsy says. But I see her looking a little worried in the rear-view mirror.

It's true that as of late, my work in both worlds of my life has been...more exhausting than it usually is. There's been a lot of activity in our clan since we were instrumental in dissembling the Hardwidge pack, a particularly brutal pack from Oregon. Our clan only has jurisdiction over Washington state so on top of dealing with a bit of hubbub over whether we had cause to attack and dissolve Hardwidge (they were keeping my brother prisoner at the time so...yes, we did), there has also been a lot of discussions on the subject of legislating some rules as to how packs operate, particularly as it involves the treatment of both mates and pups. This would potentially effect packs nationwide and not everyone is a fan of these ideas. There is also no single authority over our clan, the alphas and elders vote on decisions affecting the entire clan that need to be made. But as the alpha of the most powerful pack, I am sometimes considered the defacto leader and yet I'm not *officially*, so sometimes people get their fur up about it. It's never easy.

Still, I don't like anyone thinking I can't handle it.

"My father ran the Tremblay Company," I say offhandedly. "And he was alpha. For decades."

"Well..." Betsy pulls up to the wide glass doors of the back entrance to the company headquarters. "Yes, but the company wasn't what it is today. And it's probably a lot more complicated being an alpha these days then it used to be."

She's absolutely right but I don't like to think about all that. I only grunt in response but I toss her a wave as I grab my briefcase and get out of the car. "Have a good day, Betsy."

"Thank you, sir."

Caffeine, I think to myself as I pass through the sliding doors and into the spacious lobby of Tremblay Company. *I need caffeine.*

"Good morning, Mr. Tremblay," the security guard says.

"'Morning, sir!" The receptionist at the front desk says.

I nod my hellos, smiling curtly and step into the elevator just as the doors slide open. Two men in white who I recognize from engineering look mildly startled as they step in with me. I never miss that expression of "oh, shit, it's the CEO" on somebody's face. Even people who are the best at their jobs wear that expression when they see me unexpectedly. And the engineers are definitely the best at their jobs because we only hire the best.

"How's it going, David?" I say to the blonde guy, now clearing his throat slightly and shifting his feet. I don't know everyone's name here, that's for sure. But I do pay close attention to engineering.

"Goin' great, Mr. Tremblay," David says quickly. He nods at Samir, the engineer standing next to him and clasping his hands like he's in school. "Isn't it, Samir?"

"Sure," Samir agrees. "Godrun prototype should be done right on schedule."

That does make me genuinely grin and I can see both

3

inwardly sigh in relief. "That's great news, guys," I say. "That's what I like to hear."

They nod excitedly and at the seventh floor, I step off, giving them a little nod. "Thanks for the update."

The Tremblay Company is in aerospace. My father started it. He was in the unusual position of being an alpha wolf shifter and a brilliant businessman who could see where the tech in aerospace was going though he was an investor himself and not an engineer. He built a solid foundation and when he handed it over to me, I made it what it is today with his guidance, plenty of skill, and not a little luck. Now it's not just a small company making jets anymore. It's publicly traded and mentioned in excited whispers by people paying attention to what's happening on the engineering side of aerospace tech. The engineering labs and plane hangers behind the Tremblay offices extend out about half a mile on the outside of Quinton. I spend most of my time in my office in front of three huge screens, often Skyping into engineering from the comfort of my own desk or discussing it on a private text chat app. But I do go down to engineering to see things in person as often as I can make the time. If the prototype is functioning well enough, I think I should go down there and see it with my own eyes.

"Hey, Xander!" My assistant, Mike, hops up when I walk in. Most people are formal with me and I tend to prefer it with most employees. But it does feel odd sometimes to be called "Mr. Tremblay" by assistants. Somehow it always left a bad taste in my mouth. I'm actually more casual with the people who "serve" me directly than with anyone else. "Mason called."

I frown at that, checking my own phone as Mike pushes open the door to my office and I walk in. "He didn't text."

"Heh. Yeah, he said it's been easier to actually get a response by calling me," Mike says, somewhat apologetically.

I snort at that. But he probably has a point. Mike runs down the long list of messages which, if they're going through Mike instead of straight to my cell, means they're important but not of the very highest priority. I have a huge corner office with glass walls that usually have the blinds drawn, the windows looking out toward Quinton and the mountain where I played as a boy with my brothers and more recently took down Hardwidge and then found that girl, Alice, who ended up my brother's mate as well as making my life a little more complicated. I sit down in my big, leather chair and wake up my computer, rubbing my eyes.

"I'm going to need caffeine," I say, my voice a little raw. I really do need to get more sleep. I'm no spring chicken anymore. "In any form and as concentrated as possible. And if you're going to the coffee cart, I'd love a bagel and cream cheese."

"Sure thing, Xan," Mike says, chuckling. "Also... eh."

"What is it?" I say darkly.

"Well...that woman called again," Mike says, clutching his iPad in his hands and peeking up over it as if I might just rip his head off at this news. "Olivia Hathaway?"

I groan out loud, squeezing my eyes shut and attempting to quell a rush of frustration.

Olivia Hathaway.

That woman is the bane of my existence and I've never even met her.

"Yeah," Mike says. "She's not going anywhere, Xan. She still wants to meet with you. In person. She wants to talk about..." Mike glances at his iPad and frowns. "Some mines in Chile?"

"Mines in Chile," I grumble, scratching my scalps. "That's where we get the altanium for the Godrun..."

"Yes," Mike says. "She has concerns."

"Doesn't she always," I say sighing. "Alright, alright. I'll take care of it. First, caffeine."

"Sure," Mike says, spinning on his heel and scampering off to get me, hopefully, the largest espresso that's ever been seen.

I start browsing emails, quickly starring the highest priorities as I wait for my coffee and bagel. I click on some music. At work, I tend to go for old jazz. It's the kind of stuff my parents used to play in the house when I was a kid. It always puts me in a good mood.

Mike returns quickly enough with my breakfast and I chuck a quarter of my quad latte before calling Mason and taking a bite of the bagel.

"Hey!" Mason says brightly. "How's things?"

I smile to myself. I remember a time when my brother was pretty quiet and reserved and sometimes even seemingly melancholy. I refer to it as most of the first thirty years of his life. But that was before he found his mate, Alice. He's downright cheerful and chatty these days and even, on rare occasions, more outgoing.

"Tiring," I say, grumbling a little, and taking another sip of latte. "I'm trying to push the Godrun through. In fact, I was thinking you might like to come see it when the prototype is ready. Assuming this Hathaway woman doesn't somehow put a monkey wrench in the entire thing. Oh yeah, also I looked over the proposals Alice wrote up and I like them. I have some notes. Maybe we can meet. Then I can call the clan heads together again. Shit, and I have to go down to Mulligan because there's been some chatter about putting Didion on probation-"

"Xander," Mason says.

"If it's not one thing it's another."

"Xander...when's the last time you went on a vacation?"

I blurt laughter at that. The very idea seems hilarious

right now. I end up laughing so hard, I tear up. I think the last vacation I went on was five years ago, when I was still dating Marilyn, a nice shifter from Tacoma who turned out not to be my mate. Oh well. Things ended amicably.

"I don't know," I say, sighing. "Who's got the time? At least I go on runs."

"Ha!" Mason says. "And when is the last time you went on a run that wasn't at the moon?"

"Well...I never miss those," I point out, just a little bit put out. He's not wrong. But Mason doesn't get it. He spends his days at home, moving money around the world, with the love of his life right next to him, hard at work on her studies and her social work for the clan. Mason has it made and his life isn't exactly arduous compared to mine. Not that I don't make an absurd amount of money for all my hard work. "Mason, I hear you, brother. I do. But now just isn't a good time."

"It's really not," Mason says, chuckling. "But there's also never a good time."

"I'll *think* about it," I say, pinching the bridge of my nose.

He's right about the runs at least. I don't go nearly enough, and my wolf gets frustrated and riled up over time. Or...even more so than usual, I should say. Well, if I can get away from work early enough tonight, maybe I'll stop by the woods on the way home. My house doesn't let out right into a damn forest like my parents' place or Mason's. Sometimes I think it should.

"Okay, okay," Mason says. "I didn't mean to henpeck you. Anyway, I'd love to come down and look at the Godrun. You know how hard it's been telling people I don't know anything when they ask?"

"They *ask*?" I say, balking.

"Yeah, I don't think a lot of traders understand the concept of insider trading. It's disturbing."

"Well, come down whenever you want," I say, shrugging as if Mason can see me. "I'd like to hear your thoughts on the Godrun."

"My advice," Mason says, and I grimace because I already know what he's going to say and I've opened myself up to it. "My advice is that Tremblay shouldn't be making drones for the military-"

"It's not *for* the military-"

"*Xander*," Mason says, snorting. "Please."

"It's unarmed," I remind him.

"It's got stealth tech nobody's seen yet," Mason says with a snort. "How long before they ask you to arm it?"

"I think you should come take a look," I say calmly. "Before you make that call. The board loves it."

"Okay," Mason says. "I'll be by later this afternoon. That alright?"

"Great. Thanks, Mase. You know...sometimes I think you'd make a decent CEO of Tremblay."

I hear Mason choke slightly. "I don't think I could take the pressure."

"You're wrong about that," I tell him. "Anyway, see ya later."

I hang up and turn back to my computer only to see about thirty new emails, most of which will be screened by Mike before I start dealing with them. But I can already feel anxiety welling up in me. It's been hitting me hard lately and ignoring my wolf isn't helping.

"Lord help me," I mumble, before plunging back into the fray.

CHAPTER TWO: OLIVIA

I hum along to some unfamiliar music that's playing from my laptop and mix the herbis in my little countertop cauldron together. My kitchen's a mess. I meant to tidy up but there just never seems to be time lately.

"And eye of newt..." I wipe my hands on my apron and go to my second "spice rack", the one hanging from the inside of my pantry. I find the eye of newt right next to the goat's fur and bite my lip, holding the little jar under the light. The eyes seem slightly crusty. I make a note inwardly to buy some fresh eye of newt. The potions just don't work as well when the eye of newt is too dry.

At a knock on the door, I sigh to myself and leave the jar on the counter next to my cauldron. My phone timer says I still have twenty minutes to finish brewing before the potion is no longer viable. I stick a lid on the cauldron and, worried about it boiling over, move my laptop from the counter to a stack of boxes by the door. My crowded little kitchen that smells like sugar cookies and weird perhaps "unnatural" spices can be a bitch to work in, but I'm used to it at this point. Maybe someday I'll be able to afford a better apartment, but it's not happening any time soon.

"Coming!" I sing out. At the door, I find Andre, one of three kids who lives in a too-small apartment two floors down. He looks sheepish and shy, his hands in his pockets, so I greet him with a warm smile before blowing a lock of hair out of my eyes. "Hey there, sweetie. What can I do for you?"

"Hey, Miss H," Andre says. "My mom's got that bad cough again? And the meds are really expensive? And she says the tonic you gave her last time worked better anyway?"

"On the house, sweetie," I say, and step aside to wave him in, not that the place is exactly presentable to visitors right now, but most people in this building don't care much about things like that (except Mrs. Louis but she's a bit of a crank).

"What's on the house?" Andre says. One of my three cats, Pfeiffer, comes by to rub against his legs and Andre grins, bending down to pet her.

"That means free," I tell him.

"Oh!" Andre says, brightening considerably. He follows me to the kitchen. I've still got a big bottle of coughing tonic. Its real use is as a potion that makes a person better at math but I'd discovered a while back that it was very effective for any kind of cough. It's also pretty pricey to brew and I usually charge for it, but I know Andre's mom doesn't have any money and I'm hardly going to bleed a rock. "Well, so my mom was thinking if you'd like to come over for dinner to make up for it? She's a really good cook and she'd give you the leftovers. She's also good at mending things if you have anything torn or missing buttons or..."

"I'd love to come for dinner," I say, pouring the tonic into one of the recycled water bottles I keep on hand for giving out potions. "And I'll see what I've got that needs mending. That would be great."

I hand Andre a bottle of tonic and he grins up at me

before narrowing his eyes. "Miss H..."

"Yes?"

"Are you...a witch?" His eyes are big.

"Andre," I say, as if it's a ridiculous idea. "What a silly question!"

"You didn't say no," Andre says, his eyes yet wider with excitement.

"How 'bout that?" I toss him a wink and he beams at me, raising his bottle of tonic.

"Thanks, Miss H! You can come over any night for dinner," he says on his way out, giving Pfeiffer one last pet. "We always eat at six."

"Thanks, kid. I'll keep it in mind."

When he's gone, I dash back to my cauldron to finish this particular potion. It's my best seller, for customers in the know who come down to my place referred over by the magic shop in Quinton. It's a potion for confidence. I sell it to a lot of students and also people who are about to go on a job interview or request a raise or who want to ask somebody out. I've been asked a thousand times if it really works and it *does*. It's real magic and it's effective. I've only heard good things back from people who have used it. Could somebody function the same way with a placebo? Probably some. But the potion still works and I need to make a living.

I'm a professional witch.

My email dings. It's the email I only use for my activist work and I shuffle back over to my laptop when I'm done with the potion, letting it cool.

I have a response from Xander Tremblay's assistant. I try not to get too excited. Tremblay's have been giving me the run-around for weeks. At first he seemed like somebody who might actually listen to what I have to say about his rumoured "Godrun drone" and some of the other work the Tremblay Company does. Then he kept blowing me off. I should've known better really. He might be somewhat of a philanthropic now and again, according to my research, but he's still just another billionaire out for whatever profit he can bleed from the world, no matter who he has to exploit.

Mr. Tremblay invites you to meet with him on Thursday afternoon for lunch...

My breath catches in my throat. He's actually going to meet with me. I reread the email a few times to make sure my eyes aren't playing tricks on me. No, it's true. Tremblay's actually going to meet with me. I've been annoyed with his responses, but compared to most of the CEOs I've hassled in the interests of both the environment and human beings...this is huge.

I take a deep breath and shake my hands out, still dusted with the powdered squid I'd used in my potion. I respond politely and professionally and accept his invitation, thanking him for his attention.

When I was younger and doing this kind of work, I used to spit fire. But I eventually found out, you catch more bees with honey. You at least need to be polite when you're dealing with these people.

Shit, I think to myself. What the hell am I going to wear?

Somehow, I manage to dig up a decent skirt and blouse that look good enough for a business meeting by Thursday. My usual workaday uniform is overalls and t-shirts. From there, it's easy. Panty hose, cheap makeup used with skill, and a taming of my mass of curly red hair. All I can really do if I want to look really slick, is stuff my hair back into a neat little bun. Otherwise, it just explodes over my head. The shoes are basic black heels and ancient. If he looks closely at my shoes, he'll see how scuffed up they are. But then, if he doesn't listen to what I have to say because my shoes are scuffed up, I'm probably screwed anyway.

On Thursday, I get dressed up nice, organize my data in a neat looking folder and head out. My old Corolla is on its last legs but luckily, the Tremblay HQ isn't far. I can see it from my apartment window as a matter of fact. That big blue "TC" logo on the corner of the building and the occasional aircraft I sometimes see taking off from the runway behind it are usually enough to motivate me in my activism work.

I drive the beaten up Corolla across town to Tremblay. The Tremblay Company is in a tricky location. It's situated just within Quinton city limits although most people don't know that. It appears to be in the town of Lynwood which is where I live. Lynwood has significantly less money than Quinton. But you wouldn't know that to look at Tremblay's pretty offices and its massive R & D departments. I drive around for ten minutes before I find the guest parking but luckily I've timed myself to be a little early, having never been down to the HQ and not wanting to run late for any reason. I straighten my blouse and check my hair on my phone camera on the way to the lobby where I don't miss the receptionist giving me a quick once over when I walk in.

"Good afternoon," I say brightly. "I'm meeting with Mr. Tremblay. My name is Olivia Hathaway." I get a guest pass and sign her iPad. Then, I have to wait for Xander Tremblay's assistant to come meet me. I'm maybe a little smug that it takes him a while so that I'm very much on time but the meeting is already running late on Xander's end.

"Ms. Hathaway, good morning! I'm Mike." Mike smiles and shakes my hand. Nothing snooty about him. I have fully expected to immediately be seen as a low class interloper or something. Probably because I drive an ancient Corolla and live on the bad side of Lynwood and know exactly how much the Tremblay Company is worth.

"Good to meet you," I say. I give him a smile because I don't like to come in cold if I don't have to. "Call me Olivia."

"Sure. Apologies, that we're running a few minutes behind," Mike says, leading me to the elevator. "We're always pretty busy around here."

"No problem."

I can't pretend he's keeping me from anything. I work at home and I set my own hours. I can meet any time.

We take the elevator to the seventh floor, clutching my messenger bag close as we chitchat about the cool, crisp weather. I've been thinking about this meeting ever since I started researching all the rumours about the Godrun drone. Tremblay can be pretty secretive about his projects but he also likes to drum up interest and is pretty decent at the PR game. Or his people are anyway.

He's also hot as *hell*. Like not regular hot. Xander Tremblay is movie star hot. He could probably be an Avenger based on looks alone. I think of that now and brace myself. I've only seen pictures of him, hiding his big but defined muscles under designer suits, his intense dark eyes staring from whatever website I was reading at the time. Not that any of that matters a lick. The guy is one of *those* guys. One of those guys doing his damndest to make the world a worse place. Or anyway, he doesn't seem to care what he does to it or to other people.

I follow Mike to a huge office with the blinds drawn and wait patiently while Mike goes in to fetch Tremblay.

When Xander Tremblay walks out, I think I still visibly flinch, he's so goddamn hot. But I draw myself up. I might be a little nervous about this meeting, but I'm still confident. I've gone up against other fish just as big as Xander Tremblay and lived to tell the tale after all.

Tremblay seems surprised when he sees me too, and I can't think of why. What exactly was he expecting?

"Ms. Hathaway," Tremblay says, shaking my hand.

"Olivia," I say, smiling. "Please. Good to meet you, Mr. Tremblay."

"*Olivia*," he says. "Please call me Xander."

It's a good thing I can compartmentalize because as evil as he is, I'm trying to memorize the way he said my name just now so I can remember it when I'm alone with my own fingers for company. *Damn.*

I am sort of surprised he asked me to call him Xander though. He does not seem like the type.

"Thank you for meeting with me," I say immediately. "I know how busy a man like you must be." Xander raises an eyebrow at that and I wonder if he caught onto the veiled flattery it was meant to be. Most guys puff up a little when I remind them how important they are.

"Not too busy for somebody who's so interested in the future of Tremblay Company," he says, smiling wryly. "Come on. Let's have lunch in the commissary."

"The commissary?" I say, following him right back to the elevator.

"Well, we could go to some fancy restaurant, but we have great food here. Seems like a waste of time. Do you like goat cheese?"

"Goat cheese..."

"I've been on a goat cheese kick." In the elevator, Xander frowns at me and heaves a sigh. "I take these types of meetings very seriously, I assure you. I'm just uh... I've been particularly busy today, not enough sleep combined with too much caffeine probably. Have we met before?" His voice goes up a little bit at the end in a sort of comical way that makes me bite back a chuckle.

"I don't think so."

"I could swear..." He shakes his head and that's when I smell it. I'm fully human. I am not a shifter, nor do I have the

15

shifter gene (I heard tell of it a while back and had myself tested and it didn't take) but...technically I have shifter blood. Plenty of it really.

Magic is weird like that sometimes.

I can't shift, I don't smell like a shifter and I'm one hundred percent human. But I've learned to sniff them out, having spent enough time around them, especially in my childhood. And only now do I smell it, once I look for it. Underneath the teasing hint of high end cologne and the hair product there's...yes...

Xander Tremblay is a wolf shifter.

Well, I'll be damned.

For a second, I can only stare at him, with my mouth hanging open. I feel like this changes something, but it really *shouldn't*. He's just like any other CEO. He just happens to be a wolf shifter.

Forget about it, I tell myself.

"Um...I like goat cheese," I say instead.

"They have a very good salad in the commissary," Xander says. "With these candied walnuts? Cranberries? Goat cheese?"

"I've...had something like that," I say, nodding politely. Why are we talking about salad? What is happening? "Sounds very good."

"Anyway." Xander clears his throat and we walk out of the elevator into a wide and bustling corridor where everyone seems to straighten up a little bit when they see Xander, he tilts his head when he looks at me. "I've read everything you sent me, by the way. But I think you're wrong."

"About which part?" I say, raising an eyebrow.

"The treatment of the miners in northern Chile," Xander says. "We have the mines inspected regularly."

I can't help it. I actually snort a laugh at that. But when I look at him, he seems guileless. Or he's a very good actor. I assume the latter. He knows better. He's just trying to play me. "Oh, well...if they were inspected," I say, shaking my head.

I can already see this is a waste of time.

Xander frowns at me but he lets it go for now as we grab platters and go through the commissary line just like everyone else. I keep waiting for him to skip ahead and pull rank or something. This seems like it must be for show. CEOs don't eat in the commissary. They have stuff brought to them. Better stuff.

"You came on a good day," Xander says. "The specialty is risotto."

"Risotto," I say. Or maybe not. The place is just that fancy, I guess. "Sure. I'll try it. How much do you charge for risotto?"

Xander asks for two risottos and says, "The risotto is ten. But everybody who works here gets one meal computed a day."

"Really?" I say, taken aback. "Everyone? Even the...the guy who scrubs the floors?"

"Most of the people who scrub the floors are women," Xander says, shrugging. "And of course, them too. They work the hardest, don't they?"

"Um...yeah."

He's putting it on for me. Even if it is true. I know what I know about the mines. Xander Tremblay is definitely full of shit.

We get the fancy salad with the goat cheese and passion fruit iced tea and risotto and Xander leads me to a table by a window that looks out on a spacious courtyard across from which is the gigantic R & D department.

When we sit down, I take a deep breath and say, "I know you don't seriously believe that the inspections you require are legit? I'm guessing they're from a regional compliance company?"

Xander frowns around a bite of salad, the fork still in his mouth. His surprised expression looks sort of funny as he chews and swallows. "They are. They're highly rated-"

"They're on the take," I say doubtfully. I can't quite figure out if he's bullshitting or not. "They're always on the take. If you really want to know how the mines are run, you have to send your *own* people and it has to be a surprise visit. Have you sent your own people?"

"Yes," he says, narrowing his eyes.

"Did the foremen know you were coming?"

"I...yes," he says, sighing. "But-"

"Mr. Tremblay, they're taking money from the foremen who are probably giving you incredible productivity because their workers are most likely mistreated and they're most likely underage-"

"We do not have child miners working for the Tremblay Company," he says. I see him getting hot under the collar now.

"And I'm telling you with absolute certainty, you don't know that," I tell him. "I've been tracking companies like yours and how they delegate out their ethical obligations and...you could do worse but you could do better. That's not to mention the environmental-"

"Oh." Xander grins now. "Yeah, about that. All your numbers on Godrun are wrong. Which isn't surprising since you're only going on rumors."

"What are you talking about?"

"I..." Xander rubs his face. "I'm not the science guy. I admit that. Your emails and studies...some of them were over my head, to be honest with you. But I passed it on to my people and they can tell you exactly *how* the Godrun drone as well as all of our current aircraft are set to meet fuel efficiency standards that are *fifty* percent above the current obligation. Fifty. Five oh. And if you have any doubts about that...I'm willing to let you tour our labs and see for yourself."

"Fifty," I mutter. "How'd you manage that?"

"Ethanol," Xander says, shrugging. "I'm sure you know that the FAA approved bio-based jet fuels a few years ago. Most people aren't bothering to use it. We're going to use it, but we've improved it. FAA is on the verge of approving our new formula."

"Huh."

Xander smiles at me across the table and takes a big bite of salad. I eat some of my risotto.

He has surprised me. Just a bit.

"You're impressed," he says smugly.

"I'm...surprised. But...well."

"Yes, Ms. Hathaway?" Xander says, in that same sexy voice he used to say my name earlier.

"I don't think you should make the Godrun to begin with." I smile tightly and scarf down about half my risotto. Xander just stares at me blankly.

I think he's going to get pissed. I'm not *anybody* really, is the thing. I'm an activist and with no group behind me. Through sheer determination (and a couple of helpful hexes and spells) I've gotten a few powerful men to capitulate and gotten some press doing so and also made some bad press happen when they didn't follow through. I don't get paid for any of it. It's almost a hobby. Just a very intense hobby. I'm not powerful per se, but I'm just enough of a pain in the ass that Xander Tremblay at least had to meet with me.

I wait for Xander Tremblay to tell me off and say that I'm a nobody and how dare I and this will be a an amazing technological leap forward and-

"You sound like my brother," Xander Tremblay says, shaking his head. "Did he put you up to this by any chance?"

"Uh..." I shake my head. "No. Which brother?"

"Mason," Xander says, grinning. "Micah and Aaron don't want anything to do with TC, honestly. But Mason's my second in command."

"Don't you have an assistant CEO?"

"That's just a title. I hired Jeremy for the credibility. But Mason's my real lieutenant. It's important to have somebody who's smart, someone who you trust and who often disagrees with you. Don't you think?"

"I..." I take a sip of iced tea and clink his glass with mine. "That's wise. Yeah."

"Well..." Xander heaves a sigh. "Looks like I'm going to Chile."

I blink at him a little stupidly. "Hmm?"

"You've been doing this a long time," he says. "I know you're not full of it. I can fly there pretty quickly and back. If I've got mistreated child miners supplying my altanium, I want to know about it. Better to see it for myself."

"Right," I mutter. It sounds good, sure. But I still don't trust him. He's saying *too* many of the right things.

"Why don't you come with me?" Xander says.

Now...I'm completely gobsmacked.

"What's that?"

"Come with me," Xander says, like it's not a big deal. "All expenses paid, of course. You can document the whole thing, if you want to."

I snort at that, disbelieving. "And what if I'm right and you've got kid miners down there-"

"Then you should definitely make sure I document it, shouldn't you?"

For a moment all I can do is stare at him. "Okay," I say simply. "What's the catch?"

"The catch is that we're leaving tomorrow," Xander says, smirking. "So clear your schedule quick."

CHAPTER THREE: XANDER

O livia Hathaway definitely thinks I'm an asshole, which I'm not exactly accustomed to. Not that it bothers me. She's one of those strident types. Strident types do a lot of good in the world. They can also go a bit far sometimes. Wanting to make sure I'm not buying my altanium from mines that use kids is fair. Wanting me not to make this drone at all is excessive (unless you're talking to Mason, I guess). But I know she's not going to let up on any of this. The best play from what I can see, is to give her a little something real. I'll take her down to Chile, she'll see she's wrong about the mines and I'll have cooperated in a major way. Even if she does go to the press after that about the imagined dangers of our new drone, I can legitimately say that I made real concessions.

It takes some finagling to clear my weekend. I guess it makes things easier that, unlike my brothers, I don't have a mate. It has occurred to me that I'm the oldest of my brothers and they've all found mates now but me. It has also stung a bit. I'm often so busy that I don't have time to miss what I don't have. But seeing my brothers so happy in their relationships, I have more and more wished for something like that with a mate of my own. But where does one find the time?

On Friday, I'm packed and dressed a little more casually, as Betsy drives me to pick up Olivia. She was oddly reluctant to let me pick her up at her place. But now, as we near her apartment, I think I can see why. Olivia lives in the poorer area of Lynwood. It's dangerous seeming per se. Not from what I can see. And maybe I'm wrong to automatically put those two things together. There are kids in the street and people going about their business but the buildings are dilapidated, the cars all run down. It's certainly not where I picture somebody like Olivia living. We pull up to Olivia's building, my big, fancy car sticking out like a sore thumb and receiving more than a couple stares. I was planning on sending Betsy up to Olivia's door to help with any baggage, but then Olivia is pushing open her door and nearly falling down as she hurries down the front stoop with her carry-on suitcase and purse.

She smiles tightly and Betsy jumps out to help her stow the small suitcase in the car and then Olivia climbs in and sits next to me, about as far away as she can manage.

"Good morning, Xander," she says, clasping her hands in her lap.

I'm taken aback for a second. When I met Olivia, she was dressed in by the numbers business woman gear. That's something I'm used to and something I tend to find sexy but I put all that shit away when I'm having a serious meeting. I don't want to be anything but respectful.

I assumed that was Olivia's workaday type of wear and didn't really think about it. Olivia doesn't look like a by numbers business woman today. She wears old sneakers and tight jeans, faded, with a ripped hole in the knee, and a white tank top with a gauzy kind of blouse over it. I don't know why it surprises me. It's not a wild outfit or a distinctly sexy outfit. But there's something so easy about it and the swirling colors of her blouse are kind of...funky. It's got character, I guess. I couldn't see any character in that black skirt and blouse the day before and didn't really need to.

There's also her hair. Which startles me enough that I forget myself for a second. It was pulled back tight yesterday. Today she's wearing it down and...it's everywhere. Olivia has a mass of wildly curly red hair and it makes her green eyes really glitter... My lips twitch.

"'Morning," I say. I turn my head to face front again. "I'm glad you could make this trip."

"Of course." The car pulls out and I frown at a couple little kids on the sidewalk being corralled by an older woman. It looks like the kind of people where everyone kind of sticks together by necessity. This place has no money. It all makes me very curious about Olivia. But I can't afford to be curious about her, or to get distracted by that gorgeous hair and those bright green eyes.

That apparently means, I don't say anything at all. And it's starting to feel awkward. I never feel awkward around people. I'm usually the one in control of a situation. This is uncomfortable.

"You didn't know where I lived," she says suddenly, smirking in my direction.

"I... Well, how would I know that? You gave Mike your address and he gave my driver, Betsy here, your address. Not that I know Lynwood all that well. I spend most of my time in Quinton-"

"No, you don't," Olivia says firmly, and her eyes narrow at me. She looks a little pissed. "You spend most of your time in Lynwood if you're going to the office everyday. Your head-quarters are outside of Quinton limits in Lynwood-"

"Yes, technically," I say a little huffily.

"Not technically. Actually." I thought we were doing pretty well but I can see the agitation on Olivia's face. She is pissed. "I know you've employed some people here in Lynwood, but what have you done for the community?"

I open my mouth and close it. Because the true answer is nothing. It's something I've intended for a while. My father was better about that stuff. My energy for that kind of thing is usually diverted to my duties as an alpha. My father's brought it up more than once.

I sit with my thoughts and we end up not talking all the way to the Tremblay airfield where we're escorted to my private jet. Mike meets us. He's going with as well as a couple of other assistants who have organized the logistics. Olivia does not seem impressed at all.

On the jet, we get situated and settled and Olivia seems to be sitting about as far away from me as she can get. But I don't plan on spending the weekend with somebody who hates me.

"Would you like a cocktail?" I say, when I come over and lean on her seat.

"It's ten in the morning," Olivia says flatly.

"Which is the perfect time for a Bloody Mary. Come on. Loosen up. We're going to South America."

"Alright," she says, slightly rolling her eyes.

I make us two cocktails and sit down next to her. She seems slightly put out and pleased at the same time in a way I can't read. "What is it you actually do for a living?" I ask her. I take a long sip of my Bloody Mary. My brothers tease me for liking them. They say it's an "old lady drink." But I like them spicy and strong. "I know that pestering CEOs can't pay much and you don't work for a non-profit."

Olivia doesn't answer for a while. She just sits and sips her drink and stares at the window. Finally, she gives me a long look and says, "I'm a professional witch."

I get a little chill up my spine and squint at her. If I concentrate very hard, I can now smell the magic on her. I've never been very good at that but most shifters can to some degree. I can't think she would've said that if she didn't know about me, but how would she know about me?

I opt to avoid the topic. "That pays well?"

"No," she says, laughing out loud. It makes her curls bounce. "Not at all. But I get by."

"If you're wondering," she says quietly. "Yes. I know you're a shifter."

My face falls. It's hard not to get immediately paranoid about somebody coming at my company like this who also knows this secret. It can't just be a coincidence...

"I didn't know," she says firmly. "Until yesterday. I smelled it on you."

"You're a-"

"I'm not a shifter," she says, smiling sadly. "No shifter gene, no nothing."

"Then how?" I say urgently, instantly getting heated. "Who are you with?"

"Whoa whoa," She say putting up a hand. "Hey, buddy. You've been hanging out with regular humans too long. Magic people talk to magic people. Plenty of witches know what's happening in the shifter world. But I'm not *with* anyone. I...I smelled you."

I titter at that. "Impossible."

"Not at all," she says easily. She doesn't look at me, instead staring down into her drink before taking a long sip. "I grew up around shifters. I may not have your nose, but I can smell you alright. Not nearly as well, I know. I had to be sitting right across from you to get it."

"How did you grow up around shifters?" I ask now, no longer heated but only curious.

Now she does look very sad and shakes her head. "I'll need more drinks than this to get into all that, Xander."

I feel a kind of shiver when she says my name like that. It's a *dangerous* kind of shiver to be having around a human, especially this one.

But now I can't help putting everything together as I get a full picture of Olivia Hathaway; a professional witch living in a ramshackle decrepit apartment building on the wrong side of town who hassles CEOs of major companies until they change their ways and become more ethical...

She's fascinating.

"You're fascinating, Olivia," I blurt out.

Olivia looks at me and grins with her teeth at that and I actually get dizzy. Her smile is brilliant and the sun through the little airplane window plays off her hair and her green eyes are the color of my favorite part of the woods when I run.

I can't afford to think like that but I am...

"I know," she says simply.

Oh shit.

The drive from the airfield in northern Chile to where we'll be staying just a few miles from the altanium quarries is a long one. Again, we don't talk much but this time it's not awkward. This time I'm a little turned around. I take out my iPad and study the data on the mines Mike sent me. We've only been using this altanium distributor for the last couple of years. The metal is rare, incredibly light and versatile but strong. It makes the bulk of the body of the Godrun drone. We've also begun to use it in a couple of other aircraft. It's not *our* company that's mining these altanium quarries, it's a supplier. But going after suppliers in other countries, I'm well aware, is highly difficult if not impossible. If you care about such things, it's easier to go after the people hiring them i.e. me.

The ride is bumpy as hell and I can't help but huff a little as I nearly hit my head on the ceiling. We're riding in the back of a jeep. It's *hot* and it's humid. I wore a linen button down and jeans and I still feel overdressed. The scenery is mainly rocky with the occasional oasis of green and mountains in the distance. Olivia seems starry eyed the entire time. She looks out the window with her pink mouth slightly open as if she's watching her favorite TV show.

"Son of a bitch," I grumble, as we hit yet another bump in the road.

Olivia giggles at me and when she squeezes my knee, my breath hitches a little. "Having a hard time roughing it there, Tremblay?"

"I'm just fine," I say haughtily. And because my assistants are in the second Jeep, I point out, "I am a wolf, ya know."

"Oh, I know," she says, smirking. "You're definitely used to roughing it...in the woods behind that gigantic mansion where you grew up. I'm sure it's...arduous."

I bristle a little bit but it's hard to take offense when her pretty mouth moves like that, one fiery red eyebrow quirking up. Her hand moves off my knee and I breathe a little easier.

When the Jeeps stop, I'm confused.

"Where the hell is the hotel?" I say to myself.

The Jeeps are turning into an expanse of dirt and grass in a valley a couple miles off-road. It's not close enough to walk to the quarries comfortably but it's not far. There's a meadow of green where cows are being herded and a view of the mountains. It's gorgeous.

But it's not a hotel.

"Are there hotels this far out?" Olivia says, incredulous.

I get out of the car and slip on my shades as Mike and his assistants come to meet me.

"Sir, you said you wanted to be close to the quarries," Mike says, slightly nervously. "The closest accommodation of any kind is two hours away. So I've found this campsite. I assure you, we'll be quite comfortable."

Camping?

I do feel a little ridiculously like a diva. I just haven't been camping since I was a kid. When I want to run, I run. The woods are *right* there. No real point in camping and I never saw the appeal. I also don't see the appeal of sleeping on the ground in a tent in human form. Yuck.

"Your face!" Olivia says, clutching her stomach as she laughs outright *at me.* "You're such a primadonna!"

I'm not a primadonna," I say a little gruffly. "I just wasn't expecting it. I'm perfectly capable of some camping."

Olivia looks at me as my three assistants start unpacking gear. The weather is warm and humid but it's windy and Olivia's hair blows around as she grins at me and lightly shoves me aside to get to the trunk and grab her suitcase.

"We'll see, I guess," she says, and I'm not imagining that tone. It's flirtatious. "Won't we?"

When everything is set up, I have to admit, Mike did a wonderful job. We've got a nice pavilion set up with some tables and not uncomfortable chairs where we can eat and hang out when we need to. The tents are big too, probably bigger than they need to be but Mike knows who his boss is. I've got an air-mattress and a comfy sleeping bag, a portable fridge with water and wine coolers and other things that probably aren't necessary. All the accoutrements of camping for a rich guy who's not used to camping are here.

I guess it's mildly embarrassing.

"My tent is bigger than my bedroom," Olivia says, sipping water as she finds me outside of my own tent. I slip on my shades. Olivia has taken off her gauzy blouse and the sight of her in those cute torn jeans and a tight white tank top as her brilliant red, curly hair flies around, isn't making her any *less* distracting. She hands me a pack of some fancy freeze dried snack. "Goji berries?"

"Oh," I say, brightening. "I love goji berries."

"Of course, you do," she says, laughing.

I grimace at that and check my watch. It's late afternoon now. We'll be visiting the quarries the next day. It took us this long just to set up. But that's fine. I can get some work done with the satellite internet hook-up Mike's brought with us and then we'll be having some dinner onsite. I settle into a deck chair in the pavilion and pull out my laptop and Olivia settles down with hers across from me as she snacks on goji berries.

I'm answering an email when I happen to glance up and see the flurry of decals plastered to Olivia's laptop declaring her allegiance to a dozen different political causes, pride in being a witch, and a couple concerning *Game of Thrones*.

"What are you smiling at?" Olivia says, peeking over her laptop at me with raised eyebrows.

"Nothing. I wasn't smiling."

"Okay."

I choke a little bit. "What's 'okay' mean? Exactly? Like you know I'm wrong but you're just going to leave it there because you're above it..."

"Usually, yes," Olivia says. "That's what that means."

"I was admiring your stickers there," I say, rolling my eyes. "They're very...colorful."

"Thank you. Your laptop is very clean."

"You're saying I have no personality," I say, shutting my laptop now.

Olivia shuts her laptop and gapes at me. "I don't recall those words leaving my mouth?"

"But I know what you meant," I say. I have no idea why this conversation is happening. It just happened. I find myself wanting Olivia to like me and getting the strong feeling that she doesn't and I'm finding it infuriating.

Olivia blinks at me and says, "Okay."

"*Ugh.*"

She goes back to whatever she was doing and I go back to what I was doing, glaring as I open my laptop and feeling a little ridiculous and Olivia says, "I didn't mean you have no personality. But, you are very buttoned up. Bit of a..." She waves her hand.

"What?" I say darkly. "Bit of a what?"

"You gotta stick up your ass," Olivia says brightly.

"I'm a *wolf* shifter," I say. "There are no tight-ass wolf shifters. We're...we're wolves!"

"Maybe your wolf isn't a tight-ass," she says. "But you are."

That's interesting that she knows the difference between the human and the wolf like that. Most people don't understand that. They think we're one and the same which we both are and are not at all. "How did you grow up around shifters?" I say, shutting my laptop again. "But you're not one?"

"It's personal," she says shortly. She doesn't look at me.

"I'm sorry." I wave a hand. "I didn't mean to pry."

"Yeah, you did. But that's alright." She's smiling again, that mischievous little smile.

"Alright, but tell me this. How did you get started in activism and all this stuff you do that you don't get paid for?" I ask her.

Olivia sighs and shuts her laptop and sits forward in her chair. Our shoes are almost touching. "Do you remember Pinkerton Chemical? It was right on the outside of Lynwood until it got busted for dumping into the reservoir on the sly?"

"Yeah..."

"Well, I'm the bitch who wouldn't shut up until *The Quinton Herald* started covering it," Olivia says. "Once the people with money found out, they put a stop to it. Lynwood relies on Quinton for a lot of things like that .It has no influence on its own."

"Hmm."

That gets me thinking. A lot of things Olivia has said already have had me thinking. I like that about her. Sort of. I don't know that I like being kept on my toes by somebody I've *just* met but... also do.

It's confusing.

Mike and the assistants have some dinner system involving black refrigerated containers that get heated up on in a big pan on a propane stove and end up being pretty good. We have Greek salad and personal margarita pizzas. I end up chatting with Olivia a lot about nothing in particular and in the privacy of my own mind I note how a breeze makes a lock of her curly red hair blow around and how her bright green eyes light up when she makes a point in conversation.

When I turn in for the night, in the privacy of my mind and in the privacy of my tent, I think about Olivia, but I wait awhile to be sure everyone else is asleep before I jerk off thinking of her..

～

"What happens if they don't let you in?" Olivia asks me the next day as we make our drive to the quarries. We ride in the first Jeep with Mike. My other two assistants plus two interpreters we've hired and just picked up are riding in the second Jeep.

I raise my eyebrows at her as the vehicle jostles over another bump in the road. At this point, I'm getting used to it. "I'm paying them too much money for them not to let me in." Olivia nods at that and goes back to staring out the window. "You're awfully fascinated by the scenery considering it's mostly just rocks. I take it you haven't been to South America before?"

"I haven't been out of the country before," Olivia says. "No, that's not true. Mexico. That's the only reason my passport was up to date. I've barely been anywhere. Grew up in Northern California and then I ended up in Washington. Been there ever since. I haven't had the money to travel much." She smiles though, like she doesn't mind it.

"Maybe you should raise your prices," I say. "Market your potions and spells and whatnots to the Quinton types with money. Instead of the uh…"

"Instead of the poor people I live next door to?" She says. "Then where would they go? They need me."

Yet again, I'm both tongue-tied and feeling a bit foolish.

"Looks like we're here," Olivia says, as the Jeeps come to a stop next to a line of cars and big trucks in what appears to be the middle of nowhere. Everything around the quarries are just flat dirt and rocks. The quarry we've parked next to is a gigantic pit of what looks like rock but a flurry of people are down working in it, the clang of hammers and shovels faintly echoing as far away as we're standing. Between us and the quarry are a cluster of men fanning themselves with their hats. A few signs stuck in the dirt say "restricted area" and a parked trailer where presumably the office is. Other than that, no one would have any idea they were anywhere important.

I toss Mike a nod. We've established a kind of plan. He and my assistants are to interview the miners with the interpreters. I had a compliance consultant approve them and Olivia looked over them too. They're also documenting the visit on camera. Mike seems to brace himself, rolling his shoulders and straightening his shades on his nose before heading off to talk to somebody who's holding a clipboard and looking like he's in charge. I follow. I'm only talking if I need to. The interpreter comes along just in case she's needed. Apparently Olivia also speaks Spanish. I'm almost getting tired of being impressed with her.

There's a lot of chatter and I nudge Olivia as we look on, trying to gauge the conversation so far.

"What's happening?" I ask her.

Olivia looks at me with an "oh shit" smile. "That is a foreman alright," she says. "And he does not want to let you in."

I watch them go back and forth a bit and then Mike looks back at me. I make my way over and take off my shades.

"Hi there, I'm Xander Tremblay," I say, sticking my hand out. I wait for the interpreter to translate before going on. "I'm CEO of the Tremblay Company. I believe we're your biggest customer right now. I'd like to take a look around. I've never been here before."

The interpreter translates. The foreman looks pissed and fires off some rapid Spanish at the interpreter who calmly translates for me. "He says there has been no inspection scheduled and he doesn't have to let you in if there's no inspection."

I don't need shifter powers to smell this bullshit.

I feel it in my blood.

This guy is dirty and there's some serious shit down here. He might even risk losing me as a customer in order to protect himself if he thinks he's in trouble.

Which means I need him to think he's definitely not going to be in trouble.

I turn my head and glance back at Olivia and toss her a wink before I start talking.

"Sir, we're both businessmen," I begin, smooth as ice,

speaking slowly enough to let the interpreter catch up with me. "Please believe me, I'm not here to make your life difficult. The productivity out of this mine has been pretty impressive. I just happen to be here in Chile on business and I thought I'd come down and see the operation. I'd like to know that this level of productivity will continue. You're not in any trouble. I assure you." I smile and watch the foreman visibly relax as the translation ends.

The guy is just stupid enough for this to work. Or maybe I'm the naive one and he's come across men like me before who really didn't care how their distributors did business.

The foreman lets us in.

It's about two minutes before I'm consumed with rage.

The men mining altanium here are more like kids. Most of them look about fourteen but I see a few look more like ten, all dusty and sweaty and going at their work with hammers and pickaxes, looking exhausted. I see more than one hand looking blistered and bloody.

But I don't give anything away yet except to Olivia who sees me and just nods curtly. Mike and my assistants go to work interviewing with the translators and I tell the foreman I want to see his records.

The day is long and hot and tedious. The assistants come to me with interview notes as I wait in a chair, glaring through my shades next to Olivia, watching the miners work and glaring at the foreman with murder in my eyes. I see Olivia taking some of our water to miners since a lot of them look like they're about to pass out. The foreman keeps giving her the stink eye.

I don't know how I'm going to fix this entire problem, but I'm sure going to try. For sure I'm cutting off this supply chain for Tremblay Company. That's a given. I don't need to hear the interviews for that. It's too late to fix this.

"Several interviews reported that a lot of the miners are

under fifteen-years-old," Mike tells me. "Many of them had sustained injuries and were only treated with rudimentary first aid, sometimes leading to infection. Miners who sustained more serious injuries are just sent home without pay or compensation and some of them were children. We have more details on that-"

"Okay." I wave a hand. I can hardly speak, I'm so furious.

I think the last time I was this angry, someone was threatening to kill one of my brothers.

I'm seeing red when I jump up from my chair and rush the foreman standing several yards away, leaning against the trailer, lazily fanning himself with his hat. He's a big, balding man. I haven't seen him do a minute of work that wasn't just yelling at people. And this is how he's running things?"

"You treat children like this, you son of a bitch!" I scream in his face, shoving him up against the trailer, my wolf raging. I punch him hard in the face once, twice, three times... I can smell his fear and I *like* it. "How much money are you paying the inspectors, huh? How many kids have died working here, you motherfucker-"

People are yelling. I hear Mike stuttering behind me. He's never seen me like this. Nobody from work has. I'm sure it's shocking. I really don't care.

My hand is around the guy's throat. I want to choke him so bad. I want to shift and rip his throat out. I feel my wolf so close, I feel my body start to change almost out of control, it takes every effort to hold it back so that I hardly notice the way the foreman's eyes are bugging out as he clutches at my arm, my muscles bulging as it squeezes life from him.

"*Xander.*" Olivia is at my side. I didn't even see her come over. I'm out of my head but her voice catches my attention and her hand grips my arm. She gazes at me steadily. "We can fix this the right way. Come on..."

I'm clenching my jaw so hard it hurts but I let him go,

stepping back, and catching my breath. I feel a rush of adrenaline and fury that hits me so hard that I punch the siding of the trailer, making my knuckles bleed, but it calms me just a little bit.

This is going to take work to even address. I can't fix it today and that's frustrating as hell.

More frustrating for the kids down there, asshole, my brain protests.

The foreman is on his knees, still catching his breath and he flinches when I bend down to talk to him. The translator looks a bit terrified but she interprets for me. "My supply from you ends now."

I have to walk away then. I have to walk for a while and be away from everyone. I can feel everyone staring when I go and walk a ways from the quarry, back from the cars toward the road and just let myself sweat, the sun blazing down, as I shake my hands out and let the rage just be. I wanted to kill that guy. The wolf wanted to kill him. I want to rescue all the kids down there but there's no feasible way to do it just now. I pace around for several minutes. Mike is afraid to bother me but Olivia finally walks out to meet me, squinting, her sunglasses propped up on her head.

"You were right," I say, shoving my hands in my pockets. I laugh to myself. "I'm an idiot."

"Listen, we can do something about this," Olivia says firmly. "I'm guessing the government of Chile doesn't know about it. They're not bad. We'll go through the right channels, bring this to their attention. Raise hell. But you've cut them off. You've done the right thing here, Xander."

"What else would I fucking do?" I say, practically exploding.

"I've met a lot of men like you who wouldn't," Oliva says, smiling sadly.

"Well, I'm *not* them."

"Yeah, .I'm starting to get that." She gently takes my right hand and frowns at my bleeding knuckles. "We got what we needed. Let's go back to the campsite and take care of this." I gaze forlornly back at the quarry and she pats my back. "Come on. I know you're gonna feel guilty. And honestly, that's not the worst thing in the world."

~

In the Jeep, on the ride back to the campsite, I stare down at my bleeding knuckles. They're throbbing but somehow they help me to think and clear my head a little bit. Olivia is right. If we raise a bit of a ruckus, we can fix this, especially given how big a platform I have in the industry.

I'm still pissed though.

When, I get back, I'm still pissed. It's just Olivia and I now. The assistants are taking the translators back. When we get back to the campsite I pace around a little bit more trying to get my energy out. I'm angry and I feel foolish and naive and I'm frustrated with the world in general, I guess.

Olivia watches me. She didn't seem the least surprised by any of this.

I should hire her. I think to myself.

Although when I look at her right now, it's not a job I'm thinking of. That's a dangerous path but it's difficult to avoid.

"Come on," Olivia says softly, pulling on my shirt. "Let me look at those knuckles."

Olivia makes me go into my tent. My shirt's damp with sweat, I take it off and turn on a fan to cool off, guzzling some water and sitting on top of the trunk that holds the satellite internet set-up. When Olivia walks in with the First Aid kit, she stops short and blinks at me. I don't miss the way her cheeks redden. She's flustered and I can't help being pleased.

She's human, jackass.

I hate my brain sometimes.

"It's just really warm in here," I say apologetically. I'm not lying either. It's at least fifteen degrees hotter in the tents than it is outside.

"Don't be silly," she mutters, tucking her hair behind her ear. "It's your tent. You can be comfortable."

"Mmm."

She clears her throat and sets the First Aid kit on my suitcase and as she's washing my knuckles, being so gentle and taking much more care than I tend to think is necessary, I find myself taking advantage and studying her face. She has a sprinkling of tiny freckles across her nose that I can only notice with her this close. Her lips are full and faintly chapped but they're colored a coral pink.

And she must think you're such a stupid asshole.

"Can't imagine what you must think of me," I say, chuckling sardonically as Olivia applies ointment to my scrapes. "I'm either idiotically naive or...I don't even know."

"You want to know what I'm thinking of you?" She says quietly.

"Mmm..."

"I'm thinking..." She licks her lips. I wonder what her mouth tastes like. "I'm thinking that I've been in situations similar to this before. I tell the exec something sketchy is likely happening in his own company, he says no, no, not us... Finds out it's true... I've never seen anyone react this way. They usually try to make excuses, justify it. But you care. And that's rare, Xander. I think maybe you've had your head in the sand on some things but they're fixable. You have a big heart." She smiles as she spreads a bandage along my knuckles and I watch her expression shift just a little bit when I move my fingers, playing with her hand.

"I'm guessing," I say softly, "that you probably have the

biggest heart of anyone I've met. So big that I don't know how you manage to hold it all inside." I look down at our fingers as they move together; flirting. The scent of her is intoxicating. A lock of her hair blows towards me with a gust of wind and brushes my lips as she raises her eyes to meet my gaze. I can hear the way her heartbeat speeds up. I can even smell her desire and my mouth waters.

"I'm...not always good at keeping it all inside," she says under her breath.

"I suck at it," I murmur, as we both move in and our lips meet.

I didn't plan for this. As obvious and somehow necessary as it feels as Olivia's lips meet mine, I didn't actually expect it to happen but now we're kissing, and I'm tasting her bottom lip as our fingers tangle together. She hums into my mouth as if already a little aroused and I wonder if she's like that; easily turned on. The thought excites me and I move to nuzzle my nose against hers and open my mouth a little; teasing and licking at her lips, her tongue coming out to touch mine. Olivia leans back and I see the sheen of sweat visible along her heaving chest, her breasts so tempting as they swell beneath that tank top. She looks at me, short of breath, and it's as if some fire has been sparked and is now raging as she abruptly grabs me by the shoulders and I plunge my tongue inside her mouth, both of us coming at each other with sudden intensity.

I stand then, wrapping my arms around her as our kiss deepens and Olivia slides her arms around my neck. She's not petite exactly. Olivia's of average height and has pleasing curves; the roundness of her hips filling my palms just right as our tongues seem to battle each other. But I'm tall and broad and she's still little to me. I could pick her up and take her still standing if I wanted to. Just the thought makes me hard in my jeans and so does Olivia's mouth, her lips swollen and hot against mine as she slides her palms from my neck down my chest and looks at me with heavy lidded eyes.

There's no question posed or answered. We just sort of nod at each other and then she's pulling me toward the fancy air mattress and the sleeping bag spread out on top of it.

This would be fine if Olivia was just some human hook-up. But she's not. I know she's not. I can feel it down to my bones. And yet that's *impossible*, I'm just going to have to live with it. But not now. Now I want her and she wants me and it's just as impossible to think about doing anything but this.

I brace myself on my elbows and hover over her, taking just one moment to admire her as she shimmies out of her tank top and unbuttons her jeans. I'm at risk of one of us having time to think this is a bad idea but thank God, it doesn't happen. Instead I growl at the sight of Olivia's breasts beneath a thin layer of lace. I lean on one hand while my hand with its bandaged knuckles cups her cheek. I pull her bottom lip down gently with my thumb and her arms come up around me as I marvel at the line of her throat, my touch traveling down to her collarbone and arriving at her breasts. She arches up into my hand, her tongue imploring my mouth. Olivia is not at all shy, I realize. She's not meek and why would she be? She's all boldness and all passion and I feel inflamed with desire, spurred on suddenly. I lean back and look into her eyes as I press myself up against her. I'm rock hard in my jeans and she moans at the friction. That sound *does* things to me and I duck my head to mouth at her breasts through her bra.

I don't know if it's because Olivia is a witch that she somehow manages to get the rest of our clothes off almost without me noticing but it's more likely that I'm dizzy and distracted by every little sensation; her cool skin against mine, the addictive swell of her breasts in my palm and her legs wrapped around me. But then we're entirely naked and

40

writing together. It should be fast and probably unsatisfying, this impulsive coupling. Instead I feel as if I must savour every moment. My cock is throbbing, aching for her, and it presses against her belly.

I mutter, "I don't have a…"

This is beyond stupid and I don't normally do stupid. Not ever.

"It's okay," Olivia breathes.

It really isn't but on the scale of stupid moves Xander Tremblay is making today, not using a condom is near the bottom of the list really.

We move in tandem. Olivia is clutching my ass and the sting of her nails digging in makes me growl into her neck. I pull back just enough to look into her eyes as I position myself, lazily giving my cock a few strokes. Her eyes are so bright, her lips so swollen and pink as she looks up at me, and then I'm pushing into her and she sighs, her mouth falling open so that I *have* to bite her lip and lick at her. It's a little sloppy and rough but I'm trembling as I fill her, not from nerves but because I'm containing my urge to pound wildly.

Olivia's thighs flex against my back as she squeezes me tight, urging me on and she whispers in my ear, "You don't have to be careful."

Fuck.

I pull all the way out again and now I'm not shaking anymore as I thrust inside with as much force as my body craves to give her and Olivia throws her head back, moaning with what sounds like pleasure and not pain.

"*Yes,*" she breathes, and I am unleashed, thrusting with abandon as she rakes her nails down my back, entwined with me. Our bodies are soon sweat slicked, our breath hot as my throbbing cock plunges into her again and again, pulling gasps and cries from her. I feel myself right on the edge of coming finally but I hold back and reach down, finding her clit. It's a little tricky to do when I'm still inside her but she screams when I find that swollen little button. Her fingers dig into my biceps as she trembles and shrieks for me, kissing me as I relentlessly rub at her clit while she comes.

I'm used to carefully holding off but I'm so painfully hard now, shaking from the effort it takes to hold myself back, but now Olivia pushes at me so that I pull out of her and she carefully rolls us over so that she's on top now. I'm clenching my fists, dizzy, feeling insane with the need to come but somehow holding off. I look at Olivia sitting on top of me; her hair is a wild mass, a red halo around her. I watch a drop of sweat slide down her throat to her chest, travelling down between her pale breasts. She is perfection. Her eyes are dark as, without a word, she scoots down and ducks her head. She takes my cock in her hand and then her mouth is on me, making me cry out in surprise and I buck my hips as her lips and tongue taste me. The kicker is the way she keeps her eyes on mine as my cock slides in and out of her mouth. She sucks her cheeks in, moaning around me as if she's the one deriving the most pleasure from this and I throw my head back, coming before I can warn her. But she holds on and takes me, swallowing as I come in her mouth, helplessly quivering and electric with pleasure until I'm spent, both of us limp and breathless and almost faint in the haze of bliss.

CHAPTER FOUR: OLIVIA

I'm not lying in bed with Xander post-coital long before I heard the roar of the Jeeps returning. In fact I was lying there only long enough to think that the sex was fantastic and that it was incredibly stupid of me. I'm not usually stupid like that. But I'm also human and attracted to men and I'm not sure anyone attracted to men wouldn't at least want to climb Xander Tremblay like a tree when he's giving you the bedroom eyes, his muscled chest bare and heaving.

Now I sit up with a start and scramble to find my pants and pull them on. We don't speak but Xander gets up and gets dressed, seemingly unperturbed. He's in no rush. I have an urge to tell him to hurry it up as I hear the car doors slam. Then again, he's not only the boss but a guy. Nobody cares if he's banging me, it only matters that I'm banging him. Still, he doesn't stop me from dressing lightning fast. I wonder if he regrets it. Anyway, he doesn't stop me and we only exchange one look before I walk out of the tent, and I have no idea what the look means.

Nobody looks twice at me walking out of Xander's tent

and I don't look too dishevelled, or anyway not more dishevelled than I'd be expected to look while camping and my hair
always looks wild when it's down. But Mike approaches
before I can make it to my own tent and regroup. He doesn't
look suspicious or anything (not that it would be his business, but I just don't want everyone to know). He looks more
concerned and then it occurs to me that his boss just
punched out that foreman... Of course, he's concerned.

"You tame the beast?" Mike says wryly.

That takes me aback. For a moment I almost wonder if he
knows what Xander is. But then Xander could be called a
"beast" regardless, I suppose.

"Are you telling me that's possible?" I say, pushing my hair
back. "Nah, I was just bandaging up his knuckles. And his
pride. I think he's disappointed in himself. To be honest, I
didn't think he would...care this much." I glanced back at
Xander's tent. The guy keeps surprising me. I wonder how
else he could possibly surprise me.

"You're underestimating Xander Tremblay," Mike says
knowingly. "That's always a bad idea."

"Yeah, I guess so."

"Anyway, if I were you," Mike says, "I'd grab some grub. I
don't know if we're going to get a formal dinner tonight. If I
know Xander, we're going to be discussing our next move
and it's likely to get intense."

Just to make Mike happy, I grab some of the goofy
gourmet "camping food" from the fancy cooler where it's
being kept; dried meats and berries and nuts. But I take it
back to my tent and only nibble on it a little before giving
myself a little bird bath with some giant handi-wipes for
camping that Mike gave out. I still wish I could take a
shower, but this will have to do. I tidy up and try not to think
about how Mr. CEO is definitely going to give me the brush
off. He might be a better guy than I thought he was, even if

44

punching a guy's lights out isn't the *best* way to handle this type of situation, I really wasn't sorry to see that foreman take those hits. But that doesn't mean Xander isn't a love em' and leave em' type. I just don't see how he wouldn't be. It's fine. I'm a big girl. Just have to brace myself a little. Because as much as I hate to admit it, even to myself, Xander isn't just hot...I'm starting to like him. What seems likely though is that Xander will take some of my concerns under advisement and send me back home. Which is all that I expect. I don't expect him to not make the Godrun (although I don't know if they *can* manufacture it now if they're not going to use altanium) but I thought I'd push for it. Another drone, another destructive weapon that will inevitably end up being used to kill mostly civilians. Accidents happen and all. The thought really pisses me off but I'm often pissed off.

"We're meeting in five," Xander's voice says outside my tent. It's the first thing he's said since we had sex. Huh. Mike was right.

Alright, he'll be all business. That's fine too.

I change into a clean t-shirt and grab my water bottle and some of that gourmet trail mix stuff and head outside to get a seat under the pavilion where Mike is already set up with his laptop.

"He likes you," Mike says, his eyes on his screen. "He'll probably try to hire you."

"Ha!" That does make me laugh and I shake my head, chuckling as I idly check messages on my phone. "That'll be the day. Besides, I have a job, thanks."

"You're underestimating him again," Mike says, seeming very confident about the whole thing. "And he's very persistent."

I look up from my phone and I can't tell if Mike is joking about this or not. "Look, I appreciate how much he's been willing to listen and for coming out here and dealing with all this. It's more than most CEOs would do. But he's not going to try to *hire* me. I mean...to do what?"

"He likes smart people who yell at him," Mike says, shrugging. "Twenty bucks says he offers you a job. And it'll pay *well*, let me tell you. You're going to want to take it."

"You're on," I say, with a wave of my hand. "And you're nuts."

A minute later Xander comes swaggering outside not at all looking like he just had some pretty furiously passionate sex with me...although he does somehow look even sexier in a loose linen shirt that's unbuttoned just enough. He grabs a bottle of water from the little fridge as the other two assistants come over to take their seats and bust out their laptops. They already seem like they've got work to do.

"First things first," Xander says before taking a long drink of water. He swallows, points at me, and says, "I want to hire you."

Mike smirks and mouths, "Pay up."

Well, shit.

~

"Xander, I don't even understand what it is you want to hire me for."

The meeting did go on forever. Xander seems to be the type who gets a million ideas while talking to people but he needs others around to temper him a little bit and give him feedback. He asks me a million questions, many of which I don't know the answers to but I do my best. I tell him about ten times that he needs to talk to lawyers.

He tells me he's suspending manufacturing of the Godrun drone which was intended to be released soon and for which there has been *all kinds* of build-up and a ton of press. I'm sort of blown away. I'm not sure how he would manufacture it anyway without an ongoing supply of altanium but presumably he's already bought a ton of altanium out of Chile that he would be using. It strikes me fully then just how seriously Xander really is taking all this.

He's not full of shit even a little bit.

"Your stock's going to drop like a rock," I said dully when he told us that news.

"I'll hold a meeting with the shareholders," he said. "And also...yes."

Now it's nearly ten at night and the only ones left under that pavilion are Xander and I. We'll be flying back in the morning. But for now, we're just shooting the shit outside, drinking wine as he attempts to convince me I should work for him. It's as if the sex never happened at all. I really hate how let down I am by that.

"I'd be hiring you as a consultant," Xander says. He's sitting back in one of those director's chairs with his long legs stretched in front of him. He's holding a glass of wine in his beat up hand. He keeps absently brushing his bandaged knuckles with his fingers as he talks to me, his eyes glittering and intense. I don't think I noticed the exact intensity of Xander's gaze before.

It's a lot.

"You'd advise me on the company's ethical obligations. You'd be doing exactly what you've been doing except for free."

"I don't think that works realistically," I say, sitting forward. "I don't know that I can keep a company truly accountable when they're paying me. Don't you see that?"

"What, are you *planning* on, pulling your punches?"

"Well, no..."

"Then..."

"But I *have* a job."

"I'll hire you part-time," Xander says, shrugging. "I can see that the work you do as a witch matters a lot to you. You can still do it. And the rest of the time you come tell me what a piece of shit I am and I'll pay you for it." He grins at me.

Shit. I want this job now.

"There's just one thing," he says, his smile faltering now. "What just happened between us…"

"Ah.." I wave a hand as if it's nothing. But I don't think it was. I never feel the way I felt with Xander. Not with anyone.

"It can't happen again," Xander says firmly, looking me right in the eye. "It's just not possible. Anything...between us…"

I can't help the stab of painful disappointment I feel when he says that but I don't show it. Instead I nod firmly and say, "I totally agree."

CHAPTER FIVE: XANDER

The upside of finding out that I need to radically rethink the way Tremblay Company does its business, is that it gives me a lot to think about while trying not to think about Olivia Hathaway. That turns out to be quite a chore. If she was a shifter, this woman would be perfect for me. If she even had the shifter gene like Aaron's mate, Michelle, she would be perfect for me. But apparently she's totally human and my pack and my clan have been making some surprising allowances lately, often at my behest on behalf of my brothers, but this is not a line that has ever been crossed. What I do have on my side is that I don't know her and I've only just met her. I need to cut off any possibility of feeling more for her than I already have and focus on the professional relationship that we enjoy.

I am quite aware that sleeping with Olivia was not the best way of focussing on our professional relationship.

But I can't make myself regret it. It was just too good. The feel of her in my arms felt so right, her kisses so electric, and the heat and powerful pleasure of being inside her as we looked into each other's eyes...I've never felt that kind of connection with any other woman before. And I don't know if she shares this feeling, she might not have felt anything like that and she might regret doing it. But I'm glad we did. Because, if nothing else, I'll always have the memory of that feeling.

Memory is going to have to be good enough because anything more with a human is utterly impossible.

The rest of the trip goes smoothly anyway. In a way, I'm disappointed by just how well Olivia takes it when I say that this can't happen again. Maybe it's foolish of me, but it would have been nice if she'd been even a *little* put out. Then again, since the moment I met her, she's been striking some hard blows to my ego and I guess I can take them if I have to. It's easier anyway, if she's not hurt. And it might make her more willing to work for me. Because I really do want to hire her. And it's got nothing to do with how I might feel about her. She's smart and she disagrees with me a lot. She'd keep me in line and I don't always have enough people in my life who are willing to do that, other than maybe Mason.

On the flight back, Olivia mainly sleeps. She hasn't given me an answer on the job yet. She did seem hesitant about that and it made me want to shake her. For Christ's sake, I'm willing to hire her part-time at a full-time salary to do what she's already doing for free. It seems like a pretty good deal to me.

Now she sleeps ever so peacefully in one of the big, comfy reclining seats on my private jet. She obviously wasn't planning on napping, her laptop is open in front of her. Her face looks soft and pretty in sleep and the light through the windows is shining a stripe of a sunbeam right across her cute little freckled nose...

These types of observations do not bode well for me.

When we finally get back to Quinton, Olivia politely

thanks me for taking her along and assure me she'll be in touch regarding the job. I feel like her look lingers as we stand there on the runway where one of my company cars and a driver waits to whisk her back home to her apartment on the wrong side of the tracks. I suddenly feel a jolt of fear that this might be the last time I see Olivia. I don't know why. I only work about ten miles away from her home. But if she doesn't take the job and I deal with the problems she's presented to me regarding the company to the best of my ability there's no real *reason* for us to see each other again and even as a witch and a shifter, we don't exactly travel in the same circles.

We're both standing on the runway and the wind is whipping her gorgeous hair around and it glows red gold in the sun as her pink lips part with something unsaid. I shake her hand and I don't want to let it go.

"Thank you again, Xander," she says, speaking loudly over the noise of the air field.

"It's me who should be thanking you," I tell her. I smile a little sadly and take one last look at that smattering of freckles across her nose before she nods and turns away from me and climbs into the car.

Then she's gone.

Meanwhile, I really do have a million things to do and it's not like I didn't already have a million things to do. So, I guess I have two million things to do.

I have contacts in Washington and my very first priority is dipping my toe in the water of finding out how best to put pressure on Chile. I want to be quick but effective. I put my guys in legal on that. If somebody needs to be glad handed, I'll gladly take a senator to lunch or something. In the meantime, I hold a meeting of my Godrun engineers to announce suspension of the drone.

Nobody takes this very well. I have to tell them that the supply of altanium has been cut off for the foreseeable future. Best case scenario, that mine gets cleaned up with an entirely new distributer and organization but God knows when that's going to happen.

It's only a matter of a few hours before word gets out and it's one in the morning as I write out an email to shareholders about the Godrun suspension. I haven't even been home since the plane landed and I'm badly in need of a shower and some food. I send out the email and down a finger of whiskey (I don't understand CEOs who don't keep at least a little bit of booze in their office for hard days) before finally making my way home. I'm going to have to hold a shareholders meeting but I'll see how the email goes.

I head home, take an extended and scalding hot shower and jerk off in the steam and the heat, still thinking of Olivia's body under mine and the way we seemed to mould together so perfectly. I don't feel even a little bit sated and when I'm done I get dressed in jogging gear. I don't live right by any good woods like Mason or my parents do. That means I have to go to them. I don't often drive though. It's just three miles to a good spot near Mason's place where I can run around and feel unleashed. It's too bad that the bulk of Quinton would flip out seeing a giant wolf running through town because it would be nice to also run *to* the woods. Today though, I feel pretty good as I run, if pretty hungry. I'm going to need to hunt a bit, at least a couple rabbits although deer would be better. By the time I reach the woods, I only feel well warmed up, and when I shift it's like the best kind of stretch of my muscles. It's the middle of the night. Nearly four in the morning by now as my huge paws pound through the dirt and my legs flex and test themselves as I jump boulders and logs and creek beds. I haven't pulled an all nighter in a while and the next day is Monday but I do have a shifter's stamina. I'll be tired but I'll be fine. I can probably catch a nap in the office on my big fancy designer office sofa.

I take down three rabbits and feel a little better but when I shift back at the mouth of the woods, feeling fed, satisfied but tired, and breathless from the run, Olivia appears in my head again.

I'm in for some pain from this woman. I have only myself and my stupid heart (and my cock) to blame. She's not going anywhere and she's not getting any less human.

The next morning, I roll into work right on time as if I've had a full night's sleep. When I sit down at my desk, I see a mass of "concerned" emails from shareholders. Some of them are more upset than concerned. It's going to be a long day.

I plunge into things and at ten I get a text that makes everything seem better.

It's from Olivia.

It says, *I'll take the job.*

~

I swear, I'm not *planning* to meet Olivia for lunch. It's her third day on the job. I've had my meeting with the shareholders. It went better than I'd thought it would. But then again, I can be pretty persuasive when I'm really going for it. They seem to trust me. On the other hand...I assured them that the Godrun was not cancelled. Only suspended for now. If that changes, I'm not sure how they'll react.

Meanwhile, there's been a whole lot of press about my trip to Chile and its aftermath. Olivia seems to be diving into PR as much as our ethical obligations. It surprises me. I wouldn't think she'd give a damn how the company is perceived. Yet, I find myself reading all over Twitter about how I'd punched out the foreman at the altanium mine due to his employment and mistreatment of underage miners. The internet seemed pretty happy about it anyway, although some loud mouthed pundits seem to think I've lost my marbles. Mike would never have leaked that. I don't think the assistants would have either. I think it was Olivia. I'm just not sure why. This woman makes me as curious as much as she arouses me.

So when I see her in the commissary as I'm stopping by for one of their fancy burgers with the aioli, I invite myself over to her table and take a seat.

"Hey there!" I say brightly, as if we're old friends. I've barely seen her since Chile. I shook her hand on her first day but I was so busy and if I'd made time for Olivia, I would've been distracted for the rest of the day.

I swear she's more beautiful than she was before. She's also wearing that same attempt at a business' outfit that she was wearing when she first met with me and it doesn't seem like her. She looks a little bit like she's wearing a costume.

"Hi," she says, blinking up at me with owl eyes. She's trying to read something on her phone while she eats a burger but she puts her phone down now and says, "Fancy seeing you here."

"I love burger day," I say, shrugging. "How's the job going?"

"I like it," she says, grinning. "So far anyway. I've talked to two senators already and I didn't even have to pester them for a year first."

"Ya know, I read something very interesting online," I say, as if I'm talking about any given new story. "Seems I punched out that foreman in Chile?"

"Ah…"

"I'm trying to figure out why you'd leak that…You don't seem like somebody would care about making me look good? Also, my *actual* PR people weren't too happy about that…."

"Don't worry about that," she says, waving a hand. "I've talked to them. Besides I didn't do it to make you look good."

"No?"

"No way!" Olivia says, her eyes bright and sharp as stars. "I did it to trap you. I'm trying to give you a reputation as a do-gooder CEO. Sort of a Tony Stark kind of thing. I do that, people will expect you to keep acting that way. They'll hold you accountable." She grins triumphantly.

My heart is swelling. She's amazing. If I was human, I might propose right now.

"I really like you keeping me on my toes," I say fondly.

"I think you should *live* on your toes," she says. "It'll only make you taller."

"Can't tell if that's clever or just nonsense."

"It's clever," she whispers, like it's a secret. "Anyway. How are you doing then? Other than having to fend off blood-thirsty shareholders?"

"Trust me," I say, winking. "I'm more bloodthirsty than any shareholder." I prove my point by taking a particularly vicious bite of my burger.

Olivia giggles at that. I haven't heard her really *giggle* before and it's strikingly adorable. "Oh, yes. A wolf shifter. Of course, of course. Well, how are things on that front, alpha man?"

My heart leaps a little, and I feel weak.

Olivia Hathaway has already shown that she would challenge me in the best way at every turn. She's funny and brilliant and passionate and… I find myself smiling sadly as I look at her, taking in her scent and faint gloss of her coral pink lips. I try to buck myself up. It's hard when she's flirting and I know it can't go anywhere.

On the other hand, it's a sort of epiphany that I can talk about shifter business with somebody who's not in my family. There's something liberating about it.

"Ah…" I rub my chin. "Yeah, I have to go down to the Mulligan, there's a guy on probation-"

"The Mulligan?" Olivia says, frowning. "What is the Mulligan?"

"Oh, it's like wolf shifter prison for Washington state. It has no official name. We just call it Mulligan because it's on Mulligan Street. And it's overflowing since we took down the Hardwidge pack, though I imagine some of those men will be released soon. I have to look over their cases since I helped take them down." The very thought is exhausting. There's been a lot of talk about the degree of complicity Dax's men have in what happened with Hardwidge. The only ones I'm sure won't be getting out any time soon are Alice's brother and his accomplice since they kidnapped her and held her hostage. I'm just glad we were able to keep Jason locked up at all. He escaped twice last time. We had to build a special cell just to hold his slippery ass.

"Oh okay," Olivia says. "I've heard of shifter prisons before. But it was a different state."

She's alluding to her mysterious past again. Trust a Tremblay to go catching feelings for a beautiful woman with a mysterious past. We sure know how to make our own lives difficult via romantic means.

I scarf down most of my burger and some fries and then sit back in my chair, just enjoying Olivia's company. Or what of it I can afford to hold onto, I guess.

"There's no formal leader of the Washington clan," I say, shrugging. "But if there was… Well…"

"You'd be it," Olivia supplies.

"I mean...yes. Probably."

I'm not being egotistical. It's just true.

Not that I'm not often egotistical.

"Guess there's a lot of responsibility in that," Olivia says. "On top of being a CEO? Damn."

"Yeah, no wonder I don't have a mate," I mutter, and then wince. Olivia frowns as she absorbs that but she rallies and we pretend it didn't mean anything at all.

It makes me wonder if she does feel something for me. It would be nice to know that she does. Even if this relationship truly is impossible.

"Anyway..." I fidget with my straw. I'm not, by nature, a fidgety person at all. I swear Olivia just brings this stuff out of me. I find myself as close to nervous as I can get around her. Which is only about one degree nervous. But it's more than I'm used to. "I just have to make sure the other alphas don't fuck up and release of Jack Didion. Not after what he did to my sister-in-law and my brother."

Olivia looks up with a start at that and I see her go eerily white all at once.

"Jack Didion?" She says slowly. "What..."

"You know him?" That doesn't make any sense. Even if she does know shifters, it's hard to imagine what connection she could have to this old alpha from Seattle.

"Um...no." She rallies. She's obviously trying to cover for something, but there's definitely something there. "I don't know him, I just um...the name sounded familiar to me."

"Oh..."

"What did he do to your sister-in-law and your brother?" She leans forward, staring at me hard.

She *must* know Jack Didion. If she's human though, I can't imagine how much their paths have crossed. Didion is independently wealthy from old money and he keeps to himself and his pack for the most part, as far as I know. Though I do believe he has some financial ties to Quinton and spends some amount of time here. Or anyway, he did before he went to Mulligan.

"Oh, um…" I stroke my chin, a little bit of that exhaustion from my long night wearing me down. "He was trying to catalyse the shifter gene. Figure out how he could use it to make more shifters. He attacked my sister-in-law because of it. She was pregnant too."

Olivia seems struck by that. I would even say she looks like she's panicking. She stands up and clears her tray of food, even though she hasn't finished eating. She looks like she's seen a ghost.

"I should get back to it," she says, smiling tightly. "I'll talk to you later."

"Olivia!" I say, getting to my feet. She turns back around and I see her trying way too hard to look like things are normal.

"You sure you don't know Jack Didion? It's okay… I mean you can tell me if-"

"I just thought the name was familiar," she says sternly, before all but running from the commissary.

Huh.

CHAPTER SIX: OLIVIA

*J*ack *Didion.*

I haven't heard anyone speak that name out loud in front of me for years. I haven't heard it mentioned or heard him mentioned at all in so long, that I might have forgotten what he did to me. In some way, I almost have been able to forget my crazy, horrible childhood at the hands of a monster. But suddenly it all comes rushing back to me. It seems a cruel twist of fate that the first person to so casually talk about him in front of me would be this man who I've begun to develop feeling for.

When Xander says the same Jack Didion aloud everything starts to sort of blur around me. There's no accounting for just how upset I am as Xander stares at me, confused. But I feel nauseated. In fact, I ran out of there because I thought I might throw up just hearing about him. That pisses me off too. I hate the idea that anyone could have that kind of power over me after so many years.

When I leave the commissary, I go running to the bathroom. I'm not used to wearing heels, even these low ones, and I nearly fall a couple times in my rush to get out of there, shoving past people in nicer clothes looking at me funny as Xander sits at his table, probably befuddled. I'm sure I only made him more suspicious. It's obvious I was bothered and if Xander is as chronically curious as I make him out to be, he's probably going to ask me about it.

If nothing else, we seem to be friends. As complicated as that might be.

In the bathroom I hunch over the sink and splash some water on my face. I stare in the mirror and I see a little girl, her face a mask of fear.

See, Jack Didion is my father.

But I haven't seen him since I was about seventeen-years-old.

If anything, I should be pretty relieved. Didion was walking around a free man before. Not only does nobody know what it is he did to me for years in the name of "bringing the glory of shifters back to the world" but I don't know that there would have been any consequences for him if people had known. That's just the way things work in the shifter world. If anything, he would've been in trouble for having reproduced with a human and given birth to an abomination: a daughter who is the product of a human and a shifter...and is herself apparently fully human. Nothing could be more offensive to the old ways of shifters. Not as far as I know.

But now Didion is in prison and he's pissed off the most powerful wolf in his clan. If Xander doesn't want Didion out on probation and walking free again, I have no doubt he's going to stay locked up. I *should* be relieved. And yet...a large part of me has been hoping he was dead all this time. I had no reason to think he would be. I just hoped. I certainly wanted him dead for all the pain he caused me.

I pat my face with some paper towels and make my way back out to the elevators, hoping I don't run into Xander again. I know he's going to ask me about it. Of course, I can just tell him it's none of his business yet I find myself not wanting to. I want to be able to share things with him, because as hard headed and infuriating as he can be...I think we understand each other very well. And I've been holding onto my past for along time with no one to share it with.

But I don't want to think about *any* of that. So when I get to my office, I draw my blind and throw myself into my work. I'm only here for a couple more hours anyway, working part-time on my own chosen schedule like Xander promised.

I'm actually pretty good at compartmentalizing it. I used to use it just to survive. Whenever I was in pain, I just disappeared inside my head and went somewhere else. I don't know how I would have gotten by otherwise.

Xander, just as I suspect he would, does email me a couple times. He doesn't straight out ask me why I was (obviously) flipping out as soon as Didion's name was mentioned. He just asks me if I'm alright. I'm curt with him and then I feel bad about it. I don't think he does though. He texts me once to tell me he doesn't believe that I'm okay and if I'd like to talk about it, he's here.

He doesn't send anymore than that, instead leaving the door open for me.

Goddamn Xander Tremblay, surprising me once again.

When I go home, I throw myself into my second job. I have a long list of potions on order for a few regulars around the neighborhood. I'm thankful for that. I find potion brewing very therapeutic. I put some music on and go to work, my cats following me around my horrible messy apartment, meowing from time to time like they always do. I think they imagine I'm brewing potions just for them and they want to know what the potions are *for* exactly.

I blast my way through *three* potions. I really do enjoy this work and I'm good at it. I didn't start brewing and training to be a witch until I was almost eighteen (which is old if you're really a witch) but I took to it quite well. I might be human, but I'm a decently magical one. I even enjoy scouring my cauldron as I swing my hips to some 70's rock.

It's the next song that comes up on my Spotify that does me in. It's a popular song; "Landslide" by Stevie Nicks. I haven't heard it in a long time. But I can't really listen to it and not think about... It was playing on the radio at a gas station. I'd just escaped. I had nothing but a little duffle bag and I looked like another homeless runaway which...I *was*. It was playing on the radio in the gas station a hundred miles from where I'd grown up in the strangest and most terrible of circumstances. I'd caught my reflection in the glass of a fridge in the gas station while I was reaching for a soda. I'd stolen a couple wallets to get by. I caught my reflection and...I didn't recognize myself. I mean I literally didn't recognize myself because somehow or other I hadn't seen my own reflection in a long time. I thought, who's that ugly, skinny girl who looks like a lonely ghost and it was me. And "Landslide" was playing. And then I'd realized just how alone I was. I don't know why *that* memory is so visceral and painful, when it should have been good. After all, I'd *escaped*.

But now as the music plays, I feel tears welling up and my hands starting to shake. It's not just the song itself, it's Xander having mentioned him. And suddenly I want to see Xander more than anything. I am, on occasion, pretty impulsive. Potentially, too impulsive. Most of the time I make plans and think things through before I do them. But sometimes I just *do* things without considering the consequences first. Which is what's happening as my lizard brain demands to see Xander immediately and I find myself reaching for my phone.

I'm not okay, I text him. *Is there any chance you could come over to talk? As a friend?*

I send it before I even think about it and once it's been sent, I feel like a complete dumbass. I might have said "as a friend" but we've known each other such a short time and after what happened between us, there's no way he's not going to think I'm just calling him over to bang.

Xander's reply comes pretty quick.

On my way.

There's something *so* sweet about it. He is, by far, the busiest person I know. It was incredibly presumptuous of me even to imagine he would be free to come over to my shitty apartment on the fly just because I heard a stupid song that sort of triggered me into panicking...

Oh no...

My shitty apartment.

What was I thinking?

I gasp and clap my hands to my mouth. I'm still on the verge of panic but now even more so. I'm not *ashamed* of where I live, not by any stretch. But it's not just that my place is humble. It's messy...and humble. There are piles of laundry and stacks of crusty old Mason jars and boxes full of obscure herbs and vials and file boxes full of articles and legal documents about all the companies I've investigated over the years. There are knickknacks upon knickknacks...just because I happen to like them and because sometimes I make little potions for people who can't pay me with money so they give me strange things and I have to let them or they would be offended. That means that I have a wood vase with a goat etched into it, and a bunch of dead flowers sticking out of it because I haven't gotten a bouquet of fresh wildflowers as payment in a while (but I will eventually). I have a harmonica, a collection of antique spoons, and a shoebox full of old coins. I have dolls made of corn husks and I have dozens of scapula's hanging from little wooden figures, all from different people. All my furniture is old and falling apart. My walls are covered over with fading floral wallpaper and weird art prints from artist witches I've met over the years. There are a bunch of boxes half blocking the kitchen- those are potion supplies I bought in bulk because of a sale. And through all this mess walk three big, fluffy cats who aren't usually very quiet.

I've just invited Xander Tremblay over because even now my breath is short and I'm clenching my fists because my hands are shaking so badly.

This is just great.

In a flurry of panicked activity, I run around trying to tidy up the best I can. I pile all the laundry in a hamper in my bedroom on faith that we are *not* going to get carried away and have sex again. I pick up all the cat toys and throw them in my bedroom and run around generally straightening and picking up and puttering. The place still seems absurdly scattered and not to mention unbearably cramped and all a shambles, at least for a person like Xander Tremblay, but I suppose that can't be helped. I should have called Myra, one of my witch friends who knows my past even though I never talk about it. I just have this weird feeling of closeness with Xander which really makes no sense because since we had sex things have been only professional. Although I guess we did get slightly personal at lunch...even flirtatious. It's hard not to respond to those dark, intense eyes. I get really flirtatious when I'm attracted to somebody at all and Xander...woof.

The buzz at my intercom surprises me, my arms full of dirty dish towels and I run to my bedroom to drop them atop of the already overflowing hamper before running to the door. I buzz Xander in and then just stand there, waiting. I can't decide if I'm happy he's here or a little mortified. Then I realize just as Xander knocks and I open the door...

I forgot to change my clothes.

It shouldn't matter. I shouldn't care what Xander thinks of what I'm wearing or how I look because Xander is a shifter and I am human and I *know* that but...

I really wish I wasn't wearing overalls and a rainbow striped shirt about now. I don't look like a serious professional person, I look like...well, a totally hippie witch is pretty much what I am.

"Olivia?" Xander voice sounds concerned. I'm starting to feel really stupid that I ever thought he was just a selfish, alpha jackass CEO.

Some paranoid part of me that wants to believe nobody means well in this world thinks he came here hoping for sex...but I don't think so. I think he's trying to avoid all of that and he came because he cares which...only makes him more appealing, of course.

I throw open the door and it blows my mass of red curls around. "Hi," I say, a little too breathlessly because I've been attempting (and failing) to change my entire apartment on the fly.

Xander is frowning and staring at me with all of his intensity which is considerable.

"Olivia, are you okay?" He says immediately. "I mean, no you're not. You said you weren't okay. What's the matter?"

I sigh and actually relax a little. Despite things being a bit complicated, I feel comfortable around this man. Too comfortable probably. "Come in," I say, stepping back and opening the door wider. "I'm sorry I texted, I shouldn't have I know, I just-"

"Shut up," Xander says simply. He spins on his heel. He's wearing a suit that's probably equal to three times my rent and a big overcoat that he takes off and tosses over his arm.

"I'm glad you texted. I...I want us to be friends." He gives me those intense eyes again. But they don't say "friends" to me. "If we can, ya know... I'd like to be your friend, Olivia."

I nod and I don't know what to say to that other than, "Good. Um...do you want something to drink?"

"No, no..."

"Please let me make you some coffee?" I plead. "So I can have something to do and make this less awkward? I am begging you."

"Sure," he says. He follows me to the kitchen and I see him looking around the place with wide eyes. He must think it's the home of a kook. But he doesn't say anything for a bit as he just takes it in slowly. Finally I see him nodding to himself as he leans in the doorway of my kitchen because I've moved the boxes behind the couch. One of my cats brushes up against his legs and I wrinkle my nose. She's going to get cat hair all over his suit. "I like your place," he says slowly. "Yeah...it's you. It's you all over." He watches me pour water into the coffee maker and fill up a filter with grounds and says, "I like what you're wearing. God that sounded all...lascivious. I didn't mean it like that. I just meant ah...it's a lot more you than that stuff you wear to the office."

"I *have* to wear that stuff," I say, frowning as I switch on the coffee. "It's an office."

"You don't have to," Xander says. "Not that I think you should wear overalls and rainbows but I mean... You could wear what you wore when we flew to Chile? You had this uh, colorful flowing thing?" He makes a funny gesture that I think is supposed to signify "flowy" and it makes me smile. "It was more you than the black skirt and the gray blouse. I mean you're not *gray*." He taps his foot and he seems a little shifty. Maybe it's because I'm staring at him trying to figure out if he was mentally cataloguing all of my outfits. "You know what, wear whatever you want."

"Oh...kay, "I say, laughing a little.

"So why did you call me?" He says, crossing his arms.

"I uh..." I lick my lips. It's hard to know where to start. I felt panicked when I texted him and now I really don't know what to tell him. And yet, I feel like I do want him to know me and where I come from. I trust him. Even if we're only ever friends. I feel like he'd be an important friend, and not because of his status or anything like that. I feel like he could know me, truly know me. And I could know him. "I flipped out today...when you mentioned Jack Didion. And...I was trying to forget about it and then this song came on and I just... It made me panic and flip out again and it... I wanted to see you. I wasn't thinking ahead very far."

Xander nods at that, taking it all in as he loosens his tie. "You *had* heard of Jack Didion," Xander says. "I kinda...figured."

"Yeah..." I pour coffee into my two favorite mugs; they're handmade mugs from one of my favorite customers, made on her pottery wheel and hand painted and glazed. I remember that Xander drank his black with sweetener and stir it up before he asks and he nods his thanks as he takes it. I brace myself with a sip of black coffee before adding cream and sugar and take a deep breath. "Jack Didion is my father."

Xander's surprised and then immediately suspicious which is what I expected.

"That's impossible," he says flatly.

I can only laugh at that. "Oh, I assure you... It's possible alright."

"But you're...you're..." He waves a hand in front of me and it's not as if he's disgusted but it is as if he's referring to something forbidden.

"Human," I say nodding.

"Human..."

"Yes. I am absolutely human and Jack Didion is absolutely my father."

Xander looks at me and blinks and says, "I have to sit down."

He looks so out of place, it's ridiculous. But he takes his coffee and I lead him back to the living room where he sits on the red velour couch that I bought from Goodwill five years ago and cleared off just for him. Its seats are sunken and he's sitting low to the ground, his knees sticking up a little funny. He doesn't seem to mind that. He looks too discombobulated from this news I've just given him. He loosens his tie more and then sort of growls and takes it all the way off before unbuttoning his shirt then he snorts in derision, sets the coffee on the old army trunk I use as a coffee table, and takes off his suit jacket. He takes another long drink of coffee then and looks up at me.

"Tell me that again?"

I can't help but laugh a little. I sit next to him on the couch with my mug and take a breath. "The thing is, nobody knows the rules of genetics when it comes to shifters and humans procreating because it's never supposed to happen. Most people believe it's impossible for shifters and humans to reproduce together but it's not. It's just that, it's so forbidden for shifters to take humans as mates that any children who have come from such a union are hidden away and never spoken about. Something that's never even discussed can't be studied. All I know is that my father was definitely a wolf shifter and his name is Jack Didion. I lived with him until I was seventeen and ran away. And my mother was completely human. But I'm not a shifter at all. No gene, no nothing."

"That's how you can smell them though," Xander says slowly.

"Yeah, I just picked it up after a while."

68

Xander rubs his eyes. He suddenly looks very tired. "Jack Didion was one of the alphas most vocally against my brother Aaron choosing Michelle as his mate when we thought she was human. And all this time he had a daughter with a human? Son of a bitch..."

"Yeah, that sounds about right for Didion," I say bitterly. "He had an affair with my mother and he always wanted to hide it but she came with me... She left me with him. She was human but she knew about shifters. She said he would take me and raise me as his own or she would tell his whole pack about their affair and me, their *unnatural* love child. So he took me in and... he hated me." I smiled sadly. I haven't talked about it in a long time and it's never easy. "He hated himself for having had an affair with a human woman but he hated me even more for being the reminder and being human on top of it. He was a big believer in saving the shifter race..."

"He still is," Xander mutters. "He wanted to experiment on my sister-in-law, find out if he could use the shifter gene she carried to somehow breed more shifters or turn human into shifters...something..."

I don't know how to talk about this part. I've barely even talked about it with Myra. I've only vaguely alluded to it. Now I sum up all my courage and stare down at my hands and say, "Yeah. He experimented on me too."

Xander just stares at me and says, "What?"

"He was always obsessed with saving the shifter race, especially wolves. He wasn't even formally trained as a scientist, but he did study at the feet of other shifter scientists who were into shifter genetics. His theory was that shifters might be able to breed with some types of humans and come out with pups. Didn't work with me and he wanted to know why..."

"Why would he want shifters to mate with humans if he hated the…" Xander mutters.

"Breed with," I say firmly. "Not *mate* with. Big difference. My father did care for that human woman before things went south with her and he hated himself for it. Shifters don't take humans as mates. But *using* them for their own survival…that he could accept. He just wanted to figure out how. He thought I was the answer. He drew my blood, poked and prodded me. A lot of times he just refused to believe I was human and tried to force me to shift through electric shock or-"

"*Jesus Christ,*" Xander hisses. "You went through all that?"

"If he wasn't experimenting on me, he was just angry that I was so tragically human," I say softly. "So he'd lock me in my room and never let me go out or…whatever. It was…too much to talk about. And he had his mate and his couple of pups at the same time. But they never saw me. I'm not even sure they knew I existed. I was just part of his lab that nobody else was allowed to see. And when I was seventeen…I finally got away."

"Olivia…" He puts his arms around me and I lean into it and his shoulders are so broad and he's right there in his rolled up shirtsleeves so I rest my head against him because I can.

"I was on the street for a while," I say slowly. "Then I ended up meeting this coven who would go around helping the homeless kids. Didion was outside Seattle back then. So I escaped to the city. I didn't have money to go far anyway, I just got lost in the depths of the city as much as I could. Became invisible. I don't know if he ever looked for me though. By then I think he'd given up on me being of any use to him. I was just a burden. Anyway, the witches took me in, taught me how to brew. Turned out I had a natural talent for magic. Found my way to Lynwood and here I am."

"Well, he's not going to get out," Xander says. "I was never going to let that happen to begin with."

"I should be relieved he's locked away," I say. "I guess part of me was afraid he'd try to find me someday. Put me back in that lab."

"I'm sorry he hurt you, Olivia," he says, turning my head so I'll look at him. He's being sweet but I see fury in his eyes that he can't hide. I also see a kind of devotion and we're so close I can feel the puff of his breath. I find myself leaning in and he pulls away. It's embarrassing and it hurts.

"I'm sorry-"

"No, no," I say quickly. "I just...got swept up. I understand why you can't..."

"It's not as if I don't want to..." I look at him and see him wanting to say more, and holding everything inside.

"Xander," I say quietly. "You don't have to worry about hurting me. I understand. But I *do* want to be friends. How do you feel about staying for dinner?"

He looks relieved at that. "Sure. That would be great."

CHAPTER SEVEN: XANDER

Hanging out at Olivia's like everything is just fine after hearing the revelation that not only is Jack Didion her father but that he experimented on her throughout her whole childhood like she was some kind of guinea pig is exceptionally difficult. Of course, it's exponentially more difficult for her and I expend some effort meeting her where she wants to be. Me being pissed off at Jack Didion doesn't really help her so I fight to contain it while I order us Chinese food even as inwardly I'm thinking of all the different ways I could tear Didion apart with my teeth.

It's not as if I didn't already want to tear Didion apart with my teeth to begin with.

Incredibly, nothing physical happens between us that night beyond the platonic. That's *good*. That's the line in the sand we've both drawn. I know that Olivia only tried to kiss me because she was probably feeling vulnerable and wanting some closeness and I understand that. I couldn't let that happen. It's not just because she's human either and that's too complicated but because I couldn't take advantage of her while she's hurting like this. So instead we eat Chinese food and put on some mindless television. We crack jokes about it and Olivia teaches me to fend off her cats. It's weird how much they like me. Usually cats immediately sense my wolf nature and are afraid of me but Olivia's cats (Mooch, Scuzz, and Bender) seem oddly friendly. Olivia insists it's because they understand magical people. I think she's a little nuts.

When I finally leave around midnight I'm...a little bit of a mess. I'm glad the two of us have sort of cemented this friendship. I haven't felt this close to somebody in...maybe ever. Other than my brothers but that's different. It's not easy though and it's never going to be. Not when every time I look at her, I want to make her mine. The feeling of intense connection to her is making me want to think she's my mate and that's absolutely impossible. I feel the rebel in me rising up to insist that it shouldn't be. But I'm a realist too. I know what the clan will allow. It will not allow this.

At least I keep telling myself that. Because the voice that's telling me this can't happen is getting more difficult to listen to.

My rage toward Didion threatens to take me over the top as I make my way home. I should shift and go for a run to get my energy out but I need to get some sleep. I'm taking the next day off of work but that's because I need to drive all the way out, almost to Seattle, to Mulligan for the Didion hearing. God knows how long that will take. But I know there are a few people who want to stand up for him. At this point, it's going to be exceedingly difficult to contain myself and I'm going to need my rest.

Instead of going on a run then, when I get home I change and head straight to my home gym in my huge basement. I put on some hard rock and slip on my boxing gloves and go at the big, sand filled punching bag I've got hanging down there. I can't help but imagine its Didion's face I'm punching as I take swing after swing. My knuckles are still slightly sore from punching out that foreman though the scrapes from hitting the trailer have healed. Now I feel my muscles pleasantly flex and I breathe deeply as Led Zeppelin screams and I hit that bag with all the force I have in me, imagining it's Didion's face, his jaw cracking, his nose collapsing. It's the least he deserves for everything he's done. Yet nothing feels quite satisfying enough and I never tire myself out. It's only at two in the morning when I finally stop. I hadn't realized how quickly time had passed. I might as well have gone for a run. At least I'm tired out. But I'm still angry. I'm still so angry. I trudge upstairs to my room, brush my teeth, and collapse into bed. That night I dream that Didion and I are shifted in the woods. I'm chasing after him and when I finally catch him, I take him apart with my jaws and the taste is sweet.

~

"Tremblay." Eli Friedman nods at me, smiling tightly. I was one of the first to show up at Mulligan that morning, having hardly slept yet again, and flooring it from Quinton out to the secret shifter prison. I nod at Friedman and shake his hand. He's on my side. We've talked before. Didion hasn't even been in prison that long. The thought of letting him go after what he tried to do to my sister-in-law is, to me, outrageous. There's also no rule preventing him from taking back his position as alpha and that needs to be amended if he ever does get out. Which...he shouldn't. Not ever. Not after what I know he did to Olivia. The rest of the clan may not know about it yet. But they will soon enough.

"Thanks for coming in," Friedman says. "I know the thought of Didion being released must be-"

"It's not happening," I say shortly. "Not today. If I have anything to say about it, not ever."

The Mulligan is a nondescript beige stucco building. It's about six stories tall and covers about two blocks. It's paid for by the dues that everyone pays to the clan for the small amount of infrastructure it requires. It only holds about one hundred and fifty prisoners. There just aren't many offenses that necessitate holding someone at the Mulligan for long. A lot of things are punished via exile from the clan. But then there are people like Didion and the men who attacked my family on behalf of Dax and the Hardwidge pack of Oregon. There's a large conference room that's been made into a kind of courtroom for hearings and trials such as they are. That's where I'm waiting today as other alphas and elders begin to arrive. A few people have reported in as absent and depending who it is, I'm by turns annoyed, relieved, or indifferent. In the end, only four people out of all the alphas and elders of the clan have reported absent. That leaves about twenty-five for this hearing. Just as Elroy Finch who holds the position of arbiter of hearings and trials takes his seat at the head, about to bring things to order, my father walks in the door. My father is technically an elder. I say technically because a lot of the time he lets me speak for him. He has an injured leg and he's become pretty quiet and inactive in his later years. But I find myself relieved to see him come in. He gives me a nod and takes his seat next to me.

I feel like it's going to be pretty awkward for my dad to hear what I'm inevitably going to say today since I haven't told anyone about Olivia except Mason and all he knows is that I was going to talk to the activist who kept pestering me about the company's corporate behaviour. Then again, my dad has trusted me all these years. I expect he'll continue to have faith in my judgement. I hope so anyway.

"Hey," I say quietly to my dad as he tosses me a wry smile. "I didn't know you were coming here today."

"The man attacked my family," my father says. "Wanted to be here in support of you making sure he's not getting out."

"Good. I'm glad to see you." I pat his shoulder. I consider myself close to my father yet I don't know that a close relationship between fathers and sons looks the same way for humans as it does for shifters. He was a doting dad to us when we were young pups and now he is careful to support us while putting in his own word when he thinks it's necessary. But we don't exactly pal around. Still, I know how much my father loves me and so do my brothers. That's the important thing in my book. "Listen, dad, some stuff's been happening recently that nobody knows yet. But it's relevant to-"

"Order, order," Finch says, banging his gavel and cutting me off. We're sitting in the front row of the hearing room, all the alphas and elders packed into the long benches in front of Elroy in his big wooden seat. I wanted to make sure I was sitting up front so that Didion would see me right away when they brought him in. I want him to see exactly how strong I am and exactly the extent of my fury at him. "This hearing will come to order."

There's a lot of recapping of the entire case of Jack Didion; how he sent men to attack Michelle, my brother Aaron's mate, with plans to experiment on her and find out if the "shifter gene," a special gene that humans can carry that links them to shifters even though they can become wolves themselves, could potentially help with the breeding of more shifters.

A guard brings Didion out then. He's in a white jumpsuit and shackles and presumably they've given him an inhibitor so he's not able to shift at the hearing and start a riot. In his cell though, he's allowed to shift and he's even given room to run around and occasionally taken outside. We treat prisoners fairly well most of the time. Even if right about now I'd like Didion to meet with some torment. When he walks in I feel as if my fur is rising even in human form. I can't help but bare my teeth and Didion narrows his eyes when he sees me.

Didion is just a little younger than my dad. He has a couple teenage children but he's definitely old enough to have been Olivia's father. He has shaggy graying hair. He used to keep it short but he's been locked up, and stubble on his chin. He looks a little dishevelled especially compared to his well put together appearance when he was an alpha in Seattle. But he's obviously been well fed and looked after.

There's some more reading of legalese and then witness and friends of Didion's are called forward to speak on his behalf. I feel infuriated the entire time and I guess I must be showing it because eventually my dad rests his hand on my arm. Feeling that comforting touch from my father calms me down just a little bit.

Finch says, "Now we will hear from those speaking on behalf of those wronged by the convicted here, Jack Didion. Xander Tremblay?"

I stand up and speak from my seat. I talk generally about how Didion had Michelle attacked and further, that she was pregnant. I talk about the threat to my family. I even bring up Hardwidge. It's this idea that we must "preserve or further the shifter race" that seems to be harmful, I tell them. At that, I hear a little bit of murmuring and I clarify. We must look after our people and protect our way of life and our population of shifters. Yet this idea keeps leading to destructive and violent acts and Didion has done too much in its name to warrant his release. I hear some grumbling around me. Apparently I went too far for some people.

Well, they can suck it. Because I'm right.

Finally, Finch bangs his gavel and asks if I have any further remarks.

"Yes, I do, Eli," I say. I take a breath and rage ripples through my blood. The wolf is clawing at my door, his nails getting dulled by how hard he scratches at it. The wolf wants blood. I should've run last night. All I can do now is put all my concentration into speaking calmly even as the perpetrator of Olivia's pain sits passively in a chair next to his representative, shackled hands in his lap. He stares straight ahead, completely ignoring me. That makes me want to murder him even more.

"I've...recently become the acquaintance of a certain Miss Olivia Hathaway." My voice echoes in the high ceilinged room. I hear a few confused murmurs around me, seemingly others wondering what this has to do with anything. But I don't miss how Didion looks up immediately, his drawn face shifting ever so slightly, his mouth falling open a little.

That's right, you son of a bitch.

"Olivia Hathaway is a friend," I say clearly. "A witch who is entirely human...yet who is a product of a union between a wolf shifter and a human woman. The wolf shifter's name is Jack Didion. He is her father."

"Impossible!" Somebody cries out.

Jack looks so pissed, it's kind of delicious.

There are a bunch of other shouts and Finch bangs his gavel again. "Order! Order!" He clears his throat. Finch is a rotund man, a very well fed wolf and a good guy. I always liked Finch. He's had this position a long time because he's fair and objective in how he deals with people. Everybody gets sort of equally pissed off at him. That's how you can tell he's doing a good job. "Xander, if you're suggesting that his crime is this union-"

"*No,*" I say firmly. "His crime is not this union. It's not that he had a child with a human. Let us not pretend that such things never occur despite our old code of honor. His crime is what he did to the child-"

"This is not what or why we're here!" Didion sputters, getting to his feet. There's a rumble through the room again. The guard forces him to sit down. He looks a little panicked.

Finch keeps banging his gavel and I'm getting too hot under the collar. I have to spit it out or I'm about to shift and jump at Didion right now and that wouldn't do any good. "Didion experimented on his own daughter! He kept her locked up in a lab for years! Trying to figure out how she might unlock the secret of breeding further shifters or turning humans *into* shifters! He put the child through torture!"

The courtroom is in chaos now. Finch can't get order and my dad is looking at me like I'm crazy. Didion is on his feet. He doesn't speak, he just glares at me like he wants to kill me.

It takes several minutes for things to calm down even a little bit and finally Finch has order in the room again.

"Xander, these are serious allegations..."

"I don't see him denying it," I all about growl, my eyes locked with Didion's.

I kept waiting for him to say something. I was sure he'd shout and insist none of it was true. But he hasn't.

"Jack, what say you to these accusations?" Finch says.

"It's true," Didion says, and Finch has to bang the gavel again to calm everyone down. "A long time ago I was seduced by a human whore. She was a witch who brought me low and lured me in like a siren. She gave birth to an unnatural mongrel-"

"You son of a bitch!" I'm out of my seat and I feel my eyes flash. They must be nearly black as I feel myself start to shift. My father and two other men have to hold me back.

"Son!" My father says. "Control yourself!"

It takes *everything* in me not to completely shift and it's painful, my wolf wants to get out so badly.

But the worst part is how disappointed my father looks when he glances at me. It's like he can't believe what he's seeing.

Finch finally gets order again and Didion admits that he not only did experiments on his own daughter, keeping her locked in a kind of cell in a makeshift lab but that he doesn't regret it because he was doing it for the sake of shifter kind.

I feel like this utterly vindicated the speech I made earlier but I don't know if anyone is putting that together or not.

"Before we hold a vote on whether Jack Didion should be released on probation," Finch finally says, "I'd like to ask you, Xander, about the nature of your relationship with this human woman, Olivia Hathaway?"

"I don't see how that's relevant," I say, feeling more than a little indignant.

"Just answer the question, Xander," my father says, giving me a dark look. I feel a keen sense of betrayal at that. I suppose they could be asking because they think there's a potential for some kind of conflict of interest but I don't think it's that. I think they want to make sure I'm not fraternizing with humans. I find myself mortally offended that they can still care about that given the circumstances.

"She's a friend," I say, biting down on the words. "I think you're all aware of changes I've recently made within the Tremblay Company. She brought the treatment of underage minors by a distributor in Chile to my attention and as a result, I've hired her on. She's an employee and… I consider her a close friend."

"And there's nothing romantic between you too…?"

I can't remember ever being this angry at Elroy Finch before. Everyone is staring at me expectantly, and all at once I remember how I reacted to the idea that Aaron might be in love with a human woman before we knew about Michelle's shifter gene.

Karma's a bitch.

But I'm still pissed.

"I'm not answering that," I say simply.

I feel like Finch is glaring at me. It's like I'm the one on trial. "I'm just trying to figure out how in the course of your professional relationship it came out that you're a shifter and she's a witch and her father is Jack Didion…"

"She *knows* about shifters, her father is one," I snap. "She sniffed me out. She's not just *any* human. Obviously."

"You'll be respectful in this courtroom, Xander," Finch says.

"Oh my God.

Somebody who's not my father speaks in my defence. It's Fred Langdon, an elder from up north. "I'm having trouble understanding why Xander Tremblay is being interrogated?" He pipes up. "I'm pretty sure this is Jack Didion's hearing?"

"Alright, alright…" Finch let's it go but he casts me one more suspicious glance before banging his gavel again. "We will now vote on whether or not Jack Didion should be released on probation…"

I wasn't too worried about the vote when I walked in and now I have no idea what's going to happen. On the bright side, if Didion does get out and comes anywhere near me and mine including Olivia, I'll take that throat out and I won't be sorry.

It's tight, but the vote comes down in my favor and I let out a breath I did not know I was holding. My father, on the other hand, doesn't look relieved. He still looks like he's pissed at me. I find myself less hurt than annoyed now that it's over. Everyone is getting to their feet and I hear a lot of grumbling. I get a couple of suspicious looks but a few people come over to pat me on the back and reiterate their support for the Tremblays and that feels pretty good.

When most of the courtroom has finally cleared out and they've moved the now snarling Jack Didion back to his cell, I finally glare at my father who's been giving me the stink eye since I spoke about Olivia.

"*What?*" I say, all but exploding. "Do you have something to say?"

"Be careful, Xander," he says.

That's it. That's all he says. Then he gets up and walks out of the room.

CHAPTER EIGHT: XANDER

When everyone else is gone, I sit there in the courtroom for a while.

I've never seen a hearing quite like that before. I've also never come so close to shifting in the middle of an official meeting and losing my shit like that before either. It used to happen all the time in the old days of shifters before we were a bit more civilised. If you had a feud with somebody, you both shifted and fought it out. A lot of packs still resolve things that way if informally. I think it's ridiculous on one hand but it sure does simplify things, as long as the beef isn't too serious. But it's never been how *I* do things, as hot-headed as I'm purported to be.

I'm pretty sure everyone thinks I'm in a romantic relationship with Olivia now. That's going to be...complicated. At least Didion is still locked up. I guess I have to take my victories where I can get them. I finally get to my feet and every muscle feels tensed. I was already riled up but having to contain myself with such effort, I now feel like a spring coiled far too tightly. In the car I put on the calmest music I can stand but it doesn't do much good as I grip the steering wheel with white knuckles all the way back to Quinton. I would've thought since my dad decided to come, he'd want to ride with me but then when there's a reason to go to the Mulligan and other alphas and elders are around, he does like to go out to dinner and catch up with people.

I can only imagine how one of those dinners is going now. I'm sure they're giving him the third degree about me or, worse perhaps, my father is joining them in criticism of me. Even the deepest loyalties have limits. I know he's going to ask me a million questions about Olivia as soon as he gets back. That's for damn sure.

I answer a few calls to keep myself busy on the long drive back to Quinton and I think I come off a little curt and rude because...I'm not great at compartmentalizing. But people have a habit of not questioning that because I'm also the CEO. I get away with too much probably. I admit it. I try to keep it in mind for the most apart. But today has been rough. It's started raining; a steady drizzle that makes the drive slower going. Yet the glum weather matches my mood.

When I get home, I text Olivia quickly just to let her know that Didion didn't get probation. She only responds with a thumbs up. Exhaustion overwhelms me as soon as I walk in the door and I end up shedding my clothes on the way to my bedroom where I plop onto my bed still in my pants and immediately conk out the second my head hits the pillow.

I dream of Olivia. I dream she's still human but I'm her mate. I dream of my wolf self standing between her and face-less threats and the absolute sureness down to my bones that if anyone tried to harm her, I would kill them.

When I wake up, it's nearly ten at night. I'd intended to get a little work done. There's still some smoothing over of shareholders that needs to be done and that's not to mention the work I already have engineers doing trying to figure out if the Godrun can be made without altanium or if there are any other sources of altanium out there we just don't know about. I'm groggy as I roll out of bed and then I realize it's somebody shouting my name from downstairs that's woken me up. I throw on a clean t-shirt and pad my way downstairs.

"Xander!" My father's in the living room, sitting on my couch with a cocktail in his hand. He's been shouting for me like I'm a kid at home again. Though I suppose parents just kind of get to do that.

"Dad," I mumble, shaking my head and slapping some blood into my cheeks. "What're you doing here so late?"

"I didn't get a chance to talk to you after the hearing," my dad says. "No, I should say...I chose not to talk to you after the hearing. I apologize for my curtness."

I pour myself two fingers of the good bourbon and sit down in the chair across from him. It's my Eames chair; black leather and fine wood. I like mid-century modern things. My parents have always been more old-fashioned. About almost everything.

"I understand," I say, taking a sip. "It must have been surprising to hear me go on about Olivia. A lot has happened in the last few weeks is all. I would've told you about her at our next dinner just..."

My dad shakes his head and then he looks at me as if I've just broken his heart. My dad is shorter than me and slighter. In his day he was muscular but wiry. He was a great fighter as a wolf, quick where I'm more powerful. There were more skirmishes and wars between clans in his day and many the shifter that underestimated my father to their detriment. Now he seems so much smaller. But to me, he's always loomed large. So it hurts me to see him look at me as if I've hurt *him* somehow. At least, when I don't think I have.

"So you are in a relationship with this *human*..." He rubs his forehead. "Xander..."

"No," I say, "I'm not. There was... I'll be honest with you, alright? We had one night together and that was it. We're only friends. I assure you, dad-"

"That's not what it looked like," he says dully, throwing back a swallow of his drink. "The way you spoke about her and defended her..."

"She's my *friend*," I say, and even now I'm trying to think back to what I might have said that would have made my father think we were in a relationship. "But even if she wasn't, I would have spoke as strongly for how Didion treated his *child-*"

"Didion is a monster," my dad says. "I'm not arguing that."

"Dad, I'm not lying to you. We're *not* together. I don't know why you think that."

He rubs his chin and looks away out my big window to the view of Quinton outside. "It's not exactly what you said. It was how you reacted to Didion. It was how you refused to say whether or not you're with this Olivia Hathaway when you spoke to Finch."

"Because it's totally irrelevant to the case," I spit out, sitting forward. "And I'm *telling* you, I would've had that reaction regardless."

"No," my dad says, shaking his head. "Xander... I know what it is to find that mate. I know what it is to stumble on that person without whom you feel you cannot even live. That connection and that possessiveness it ignites in the wolf... That's what I saw." He points to his own eyes with two fingers. "I saw it here. Saw it right in your eyes."

"Dad," I say softly. I don't even know how to follow it up but I feel a chill in my blood. This *can't* happen. It's impossible.

"I know it's not your fault, how you feel," my dad says

slowly. "It's been known to happen. The fates can be cruel. Many have fallen under the enchantment of finding a true mate and yet the relationship proved to be impossible. You must resist this, son."

"I-I know, I'm not...I'm not..." I rub my face. I'm not like this with anyone but my father. Maybe that's how it should be, but I really hate it sometimes. "I didn't ask for this."

There it is. I've finally admitted it out loud. The words bubbling out of me and utterly out of my control. It's a kind of relief and also...incredibly not. Because now it's real.

"I know that," my dad says, patting my back. "But I'm concerned here. You need to cut her out of your life. That's the only way forward. This friendship? Her working for you? This can't continue."

Now my shoulders tense up and I look at him, disbelieving. "I'm not cutting her out," I say, the words like poison. "And I'm certainly not firing her."

"You're showing a lack of wisdom," my dad says sadly. "After this nonsense with the Godrun-"

"*Nonsense?*" I say, jumping to my feet. "I suspended the Godrun because the materials were being mined by abused *children-*"

"You punched the foreman?" My dad says, raising his voice as he stands up. "You suspended manufacturing before any kind of investigation? Before bringing it to your board-"

"You're goddamn right I did!" I say, all but exploding in my father's face.

"Your stock is dropping," my dad says, practically hissing. "Stock in the company that *I* built, Xander, not you."

"Okay," I say, nodding. "I get it. You're worried about your company that I've built up into the powerhouse it is-"

"You are spiralling-"

"I did the right thing and you're talking about the *stock*," I say, spiteful and not a little bit astonished.

"I don't begrudge your motive," he says. "Only the way you did it. Hot-headed and reckless and stubborn as always."

"I've run this pack and this company and frankly this *family* since I was practically a teenager," I say, clenching my fists as I step into his space. "I've always done what was best for the pack and for you and mom and my brothers and the clan and goddammit I work so hard I can't see straight! I can't... I'm the oldest of my brothers and I don't have a mate? Why do you think that is? Because all I do all day is for everyone else!"

"That's your duty!"

"And I've never complained!" I shout, and suddenly my glass is hitting the wall and shattering everything exploding out of me. "I didn't complain *ever* when I had to go learn how to be an alpha while my brothers got to have fun and I didn't complain when I had to take over Tremblay Company instead of studying what I felt like studying. I've done *everything...*" I feel a lump in my throat and I choke it down, swallowing painfully but my eyes are welling up. "And now I'm telling you that I'm willing to sacrifice this...this...love of a human... And why? I don't know! I don't know why!" I find myself laughing a little hysterically now as my dad only stares at me like I'm crazy. "I don't understand *why* I can't be with her. Because of some rule written so long ago that nobody remembers who even thought of it." I shake my head and wipe my eyes, rebellious tears having spilled to my mortification.

"I believe this relationship with this Hathaway woman is affecting your decision making as an alpha." My dad speaks so calmly that it pisses me off further. I want him to be upset like I am. Suddenly resentments that I didn't know I possessed are all rising to the surface, catalysed by my father's apparent disappointment in me. "Pull yourself together and start making some real changes. Fix the company and get rid of this Olivia Hathaway or I don't know, Xander... We may have to think about one of your brother's taking over. And if one of them doesn't, I will."

"You can't be serious," I whisper. I feel sick. The thought of being *deposed* as alpha would be...beyond humiliating. It only happens in pretty extreme circumstances. And that's not to mention that I truly love being the alpha. I love it more than running the company which I sometimes love and often despise but I'm generally just used to it. It's just my duty. It's just my life. It always has been. "You wouldn't vote me out, you'd have to... That would be a clan decision. Dad, I'd be a laughing stock. It would... You *can't*."

"If you continue to run things like this," my dad says slowly, "we're going to start losing allies. You're making too many mistakes, Xander I have to stop you before you start causing some real harm. Things have been so turbulent lately after Didion and Hardwidge... And now Alice wants all these new rules."

My mouth twists at that. I didn't realize my dad had a problem with it. "Dad, she's doing that to stop another Hardwidge-"

"I know *why*," he says. "But it's making a lot of the old men like me pretty unhappy. Dictating how packs are run. This is a fragile time. And you're acting like a goddamn wild card."

"Dad-"

"We're done," he snaps. And suddenly I'm a teenager again. I feel like I was just grounded.

Except that I'm *not* a teenager.

"*Hey*," I snap, my alpha hackles rising. I may be upset but I still run this fucking pack. "You're old and you're broken down and you're feckless, dad. Try to take me down and see what happens."

We exchange a hard look and he sees I'm not kidding.

Nothing else is said and for the second time that day, my dad walks away from me. This time he slams the door on his way out.

~

It's when Aaron calls me that I really start to lose my shit.

Dad has talked to him about Olivia and he calls to read me the riot act. How could I be in love with a human after how I acted about him and Michelle? How am I such a hypocrite?

I'm so angry at this point, I can hardly speak and I hang up on my brother mid-sentence. That earns me a text from Mason just a few minutes later. He wants to know what in the name of God is going on. I can only imagine what he's heard.

Then something happens that hasn't happened to me since my first year as CEO of Tremblay Company. It used to happen to me all the time. Though I never told a single soul about it.

I have a fucking anxiety attack. As old fashioned as shifters can be about things like mating with humans, they're even more old fashioned about certain afflictions like anxiety or depression that *they* believe only affect humans. But I well know that's not true because...I have anxiety. I suppose I could blame my mother and her humanity despite her shifter gene for it but it hardly matters. Either way, I could never let anyone see what I thought of as weakness. I thought it had gone away though; a symptom of my youth. But now here I am, my heart pounding much to fast and a feeling like I can't breathe. I feel like I'm going to *die*. It's all piled on me suddenly and it's like a goddamn freight train, this feeling.

It takes me an hour to talk myself down, it using all the old coping mechanisms I used to use. I tell myself this feeling

XANDER'S MATE

is temporary and try to breathe. I listen to music and drink ice water, holding the cold glass in my hands because it grounds me. I go on a jog around the block a few times, just enough to release some endorphins. When I come back I do feel a little better. When I was younger, I tried to shift my way out of it, sure that the wolf was the answer to any problem. But that never helped. My problem was a human one. But I was too ashamed to tell anybody.

When I feel better, there's only one place I want to be. It's a bad idea but I'm out of good ones and I'm not much feeling like the alpha who knows all right now.

It's pouring rain in Lynwood when I get there. The buzzer at Olivia's building's front door has two vertical rows of buttons, one for each residence. The top two buttons stare at me like eyes. I feel as if they're accusing me of something. I don't have an umbrella and I'm going to get soaked quick yet I just stand there for a minute. The rain is cold and I didn't even think to bring a coat. I'm wearing a white t-shirt and exorbitantly expensive trousers as I stand there in the pouring rain. But I can smell her. Even down here I can pick her out among all the humans in the building and I shiver as I feel that connection to her thrumming as if there's an electric thread between us. I know that the way I'm feeling, after this shitty day, if I public that thought...the idea of being "just friends" is going right out the window.

I'm the alpha, I'm the CEO and I'm the Tremblay who's supposed to have it all under control and right at this moment...I don't care about any of it.

I push the button next to the name Hathaway to buzz and a moment later a squelchy voice says, "Hello?"

"Olivia, it's me," I say, pressing the button again.

"Oh!" There's a pause and some white noise and Olivia says, "Xander, what're you doing here?"

"I'm sorry, it's late," I say, my cheeks burning even in

91

frigid downpour. "I just...I... I need to see you? I need..." I swallow. There's no point in pretending anymore.

Tell her.

Tell her.

"Olivia, I *need* you."

There's a *long* pause then but I'm not going anywhere. Not now.

"But you..." Olivia sounds as scared as I am. "You said...What do you mean?"

"I mean I *need* you."

She knows what I mean. I can feel that she knows somehow, now that I'm not trying to push these feelings away, it's all coming rushing into me; the absolute assurance that Olivia Hathaway is both a human and my mate.

I don't hear anything else and I don't say anything else. I wonder if she's not going to let me in and step down to the street, staring up at her window where I can see the lights are on. I'm not going to hold up a boombox or anything but I don't plan on going anywhere for a bit. Because somehow just standing here in the rain, in the dark, on the street in a sketchy area of Lynwood, right here under Olivia's window is making me feel better than I have all day even given the absolute reality that I could start a war by calling this woman mine. I see her window open on the third floor and Olivia's little head under that mass of red hair pops out. She looks down at me, astonished. She looks like she wants to say something but she doesn't. She goes back in and shuts the window and I wait some more. I stand on the sidewalk and let the rain soak me and close my eyes, just breathing.

When I hear the front door open, I don't even assume it's her. But I open my eyes and there she is. She's wearing a tank top and pink pyjama pants and she's quickly getting soaked.

"What are you doing here?" She says, sounding breathless. She must have just run down the stairs.

"I…" I shake my head. Alpha CEO Xander who's always in control stutters and feels helpless. "I don't know what to do. I love you. I'm in love with you."

"Xander…"

"I know."

"You *can't*. I know you can't-"

"Your father was a shifter-"

"I'm still *human* by any measure that matters. You can't."

"I know I can't," I say, stepping towards her. The streetlights are making her dampening red curls glitter like red gold. I love it when her hair looks like that. I love how the raindrops fall on her lips. I love that she's wearing a rainbow bracelet and I love that she wears overalls and I love that she makes potions for people in trade for useless things and I love that she works so hard to try to make this world a better place and I love how she smiles and I love her.

"I don't care," I say, before cupping her cheeks between my palms and kissing her.

It's not like in Chile. Although there's nothing like kissing the woman you love for the first time. This is something else. It's deeper and slower and even though I seem to be acting recklessly, I'm *sure* and I kiss her with all my assurance. I kiss her like I never want to stop. I'm cold and soaking wet but Olivia's mouth is hot as it slides against mine. Her lips part and I stroke her pale cheeks with my thumbs as I lick inside her and she gasps a little and grabs fistfuls of my drenched t-shirt, pulling me closer.

"I don't know what to do," I say, resting my forehead against hers. "Everything feels like it's falling apart but all I know is I love you. You're my mate. I feel it in my bones. Tell me you don't feel it too and I'll go and I'll never mention this again-"

"I feel it," she whispers. "Of course, I do."

I taste her top lip and her bottom lip and I wrap my arms

around her as our tongues curl together. I feel her shudder in my arms and I lean back, both of us breathless.

"I'm sorry," I mumble, rubbing her arms. "You're cold. You don't have to-"

"I love you too," she says. I make a funny little yelp of a noise and I kiss her once more. "Come upstairs," she says, pulling on my arms. "Come upstairs with me."

Olivia tugs on my hand and I stumble after her, up the front stoop and inside and up three flights of stairs to her door where I can't wait to take her in my arms again. We make out sloppily, leaning against her door until we hear someone else's door open and Olivia gasps a little, breaking away to let us into her place.

Olivia's place is messy. Well, it's *cluttered* anyway with faded old wallpaper and crookedly hung pictures and weird knicknacks taking up space on seemingly every empty surface. But it's *warm* and it's a home. My own place is beautiful and impeccably designed but this place is Olivia all over and I love that about it. Now she tugs me forward, our lips still locked as if we might suffocate should we break apart.

But then she does. We're standing in her living room, so close to the bedroom. I need to be with her. I need her in my arms. It feels like an absolute physical necessity. I want to feel that connection to her. I want to feel like we're the same person. I want it more than I've ever wanted anything in my life. My wolf is howling within me. I want her to be *mine* and I want to show her that I'm hers.

"Are you okay, Xander?" She wraps her arms around my neck and gazes at me with worried eyes. I tangle my fingers in her hair; all that gorgeous hair in tight little coils.

"Not really," I say, and it feels alright admitting it. "But I'm not here for you to make me feel better. I'm here because I know that fighting this is a losing battle. Because I love you. Nothing can stop that. Nothing."

Olivia holds me tighter and she stands on her tiptoes, her gaze roving over my face as I wrap my arms around her again. "Take me to bed," she whispers.

I lift her right off her feet and she wraps her legs around me and I haul her into her bedroom. Olivia's bedroom is even more cluttered than the rest of her place but that's hardly what I'm thinking about as I all but toss her onto the hastily made bed and climb onto top of her. Her hand seems a little smaller when I see those pale fingers wrap around my biceps. Olivia isn't small, but I'm about 6'3 and packed with not very small muscles. They're muscles that Olivia seems to be taking some pleasure in just now as I hover over her. She bites her lip as she looks up at me, squeezing my biceps and then sliding her hands down the planes of my chest to press at my quivering abs through my soaked shirt. My hair is a mess, dark dripping locks flopping over into my eyes and I watch one raindrop fall onto Olivia's pale throat and slide down to the V of her chest, slipping down into the shadow between her breasts. She wraps her legs around me and the slide of her warms legs against my soaking trousers that cling to my skin is driving me mad. For a while we only kiss and writhe together but I can *feel* it; the two of us becoming one. This is what having a mate must be. And now I understand what all my brothers have fought for. Just this. All this.

I sit back on my heels and take Olivia's hands to sit up with me so I can help her take off her damn shirt and she scrambles to peel mine off my body, haphazardly throwing it into a corner where it lands with a wet splat. She unbuckles my belt and unzips my fly but I get impatient to feel her body under mine again and I push her down onto the bed, climbing on top of her. My cock feels painfully hard as Olivia shoves my trousers down and her hot hands slide inside my briefs as I feel her fingers wrap around me. I gasp against her neck, sucking a mark there. I'd love to truly mark her. But now is not the time for that. She gives me a few slow, warm strokes and then helps to shove my pants down off my legs and I kick them off to the floor.

Our lovemaking this time is slow and sweet. For a while we just move together, feeling each other, inspecting every inch of each other's damp skin. I find scars on her upper arm and by the sadness in her eyes, I know they must be Didion's doing so I kiss them as she squeezes me tight. She explores every inch of the planes of my chest with her mouth once she's rolled us over, straddling me, forcing me to wait for her. I tangle my fingers in her hair, luxuriating in that pleasing, silky springiness. When she nibbles on one of my nipples I laugh even as I moan and she smiles up at me through that curtain of hair. Then she's stroking me while she licks and bites at my chest and all I can do is take her ass in both hands, squeezing the pleasing and creamy flesh I find there.

"Kiss me, sweetheart," I mutter and Olivia indulges me, moving up so that my cock is pressing against her and it throbs, my desire craving her. Olivia moves, positioning herself, taking control and then all at once I'm inside her as her mouth covers mine again.

Olivia rides me, bracing her hands on my chest and I'm so taken with the beauty of her and helpless with pleasure that I can't speak. I slide my hand from her belly to her breasts and she captures it, kissing my palm, hugging my arms as she rocks into me, panting as she sucks on my fingers. I buck up into her and our eyes lock as our connections makes us one person, one soul joined and then I'm coming, coming, joined in love with my mate...

CHAPTER NINE: JACK

his is what I get for trying to save our kind.

I pace in my cell. The room is long and it has a few high benches built into the walls. The Mulligan cells were intentionally built to allow shifter prisoners room to shift and pace and climb around to some extent. It is still extremely unpleasant for the average wolf who is used to being able to run in the woods and feel the wind at his back. There are no trees to smell in the cells of Mulligan. There are no creeks to stomp through and no rabbits to hunt. That's the point though after all. I am supposed to be contained and restricted. I'm supposed to be paying penance for what I have done. I am supposed to be feeling remorse.

Yet, I feel none.

Everything I have done, I have done in the name of preserving not just the way of life of shifters but our existence itself. If I have failed, it was not for lack of trying. But I cannot regret following the code that has been our dictate for so many generations. Loyalty to the pack and to the clan above all. What could be more loyal than attempting, by *any* means necessary, to find a way to bring more shifters into the world? Our population has been decreasing for generations. If the answer to that problem can be found by using a few humans or humans with the so-called "shifter gene" for my purposes, then so be it. I can't apologize for wanting so desperately to save my people.

These are thoughts that run through my mind over and over as I pace back and forth in my cell. I spend a lot of time shifted. On some level it's more infuriating to feel so contained as the wolf, but it can be easier to be comfortable too. Human bodies are so fragile. On either side of me are more cells. Most of them are peopled by prisoners taken during the raid on the Hardwidge encampment. Yet another Tremblay bitch was involved in that boondoggle. How many good wolves will end up locked away in this torturous enclosure, unjustly imprisoned for the crime of wanting only the best for shifter kind, all because one of the Tremblays fell in love? And worse, now there's word that one of them wants new laws dictating how packs are run. Mason Tremblay's mate, an "innocent" escapee from Hardwidge, wants to help Xander decide how packs should run themselves. Supposedly, it would be in the name of protecting mates and pups, to prevent another Hardwidge. But the truth is too obvious. Wolves like the Tremblays are more human than shifter. They only want to protect themselves and they would control how every other shifter lives, mandating them to be more like humans. I can only imagine that mating with humans is next, as far as they've gone with it. They already mate with those humans with the "shifter gene." Shifter gene, my ass. Michelle Tremblay is as human as any bitch off the street without that gene. She can't shift, than she's not a wolf. That much is obvious.

The Tremblays will ruin us all.

I won't lie. I am obsessed with that truth. It's all I can think about in this cage. Xander Tremblay somehow stumbling upon Olivia is only the icing on the cake. I don't know how she found him or how he found her. It must have been deliberate. He set out to ruin me, to keep me locked up here because I dared to attempt to find a path forward for shifter kind.

There is only one answer to this nightmare future the Tremblays would create.

I must destroy them. How I will do that from this cell is the question. But there is no other option. I have been plotting how though. There's nothing else to think about in here anyway. If I'd been granted probation, I would've been pounding the pavement seeking allies and putting an agenda together. As it is, my only option is to find allies here and plot an escape. After that...the sky's the limit.

I've been speaking to the other prisoners. Everyone near me is from Hardwidge. I always thought of them as a trash pack but in truth, they have had the right idea all along. They were true to their principles of living like wolves. We all should be following their example, not trying not to prevent another pack like them. The only wolf who will not speak to me is Jason. From what I've gathered, he's the brother of the girl who escaped Hardwidge and ended up with Mason Tremblay and is now trying to impose these fascistic new rules. Jason won't give me the time of day. He won't speak to anyone in fact. It's too bad. He's managed to escape Mulligan before and I don't know how he did it. Now he's back, in a cell across from me. He never speaks to anyone, he only sulks in his cell. He even seems remorseful. He's a useless wolf then. And too weak to be of any real use.

"Kyle?" I'm shifted back into human form, clutching the bars of my cell. To my right is Kyle. He was Jason's lackey from what I gather. Jason won't even talk to him now. I can tell Kyle is pissed about it. When Kyle isn't shifted he's sitting up against the bars and often yelling pretty colorful insults at Jason who just sits there, staring and taking it. "Hey, Kyle."

I've spoke to Kyle a bit. He seems wary of me as a "city shifter." But Hardwidge wolves are always suspicious of anyone from another pack. To some degree though, he does seem to respect me just for having been an alpha.

"Yeah?" Kyle was standing up and now he sits on the bench against the bars between us, rubbing his eyes tiredly. "What, Jack?"

"I've been thinking..."

"I'll bet you have," Kyle says, cackling a little. "Probation hearing didn't go so well, huh?"

"No," I say darkly. "No surprise there. Most people are in the pocket of Xander Tremblay. But there were some votes in my favor."

Kyle gives me a long look. I get the impression he wasn't much more than a yes man toadie for Jason. That's good. I can exploit that. "What do you want, Jack?"

"Me and everyone who fought for the Hardwidge pack want the same thing," I say slowly. "We want wolves to act like wolves and not humans. We want to preserve our kind."

"We want to take down the Tremblays," I say smirking a little. He turns toward me, gripping the bars. He's paying attention now.

"Listen, I've got allies on the outside," I tell him. "Hardwidge doesn't. Because people didn't understand it. But they *could*. What you do have is numbers where it counts. Right here in Mulligan."

"You want to plot an escape," Kyle says, whispering.

"I want to plot an escape," I say, nodding. "And then I want to form an army. And if you're saying that you're on board, I need to know that you don't mind getting your hands dirty when it comes to the Tremblays or anyone who would defend them?"

"Dirty?" Kyle licks his teeth and cackles. "Well, I know an explosives guy Dax always meant to use if things had gone the way they were supposed to. How's that for dirty? All I need to do is make a call once we're out."

"That's good," I say, nodding. "'That's real good. Now about this escape…"

"It wouldn't even be hard," Kyle says, glancing around to make sure nobody's listening. "Mulligan isn't used to so many prisoners. They don't have the manpower to stop a mass breakout. It would be messy as hell, but it can be done. Just gotta put the word out."

I look at him steadily and say, "Then put the goddamn word out."

CHAPTER TEN: OLIVIA

When I wake up in Xander's arms, nothing seems even slightly out of place. It should, I guess. A few days ago, I would have thought waking up in Xander's arms would mean that one or both of us would immediately panic. I would have thought he'd get skittish or cold just like he did in Chile, and say that this can't happen again. And then I'd pretend that it was fine. But all that's over now. I'm sure of it as he spoons up behind me. I hear him stir and I feel his warm breath on the back of my neck, his arms around me as his body presses up against mine.

He's mine.

"Your bed's comfy," he murmurs.

"I hope so," I say, playing with his hand where it clasps mine. "I sleep in it every night."

"No, I mean...my bed was so expensive," he says into my skin. His goatee pleasantly tickles my neck and I shiver. "But it wasn't worth the money. Yours is just as good."

"Good to know," I say, chuckling.

"It might be the woman I'm holding onto that makes me like it so much," he says. If I didn't know better, I'd think he sounds just a little bit tentative. It's as if he's asking for confirmation that this is as real to me as it is to him.

"It *might* be," I say, smiling to myself and playing coy.

"Oliviaaaa," he says, singing a little bit.

I roll over in bed to face him. There's always something sweet (or anyway there should be) about waking up in somebody's arms in the morning. There's not time for makeup or even to get rid of the morning breath and wash your face. Your hair is messy and you probably have wrinkling from pillows pressing into your skin. I look in Xander's eyes and smile slyly as I reach up to press my fingers to a pillow crease in his cheek.

"You look beautiful in the morning," he says softly. He plays with my hair, twirling a lock around his finger. "You look beautiful in the afternoon and in the evening and at four o'clock in the morning. I love the way you look. I love *you*."

"Am I your mate?" I whisper.

"Fucking hell yes, you are," he says before pressing a kiss to my neck. One kiss becomes three and then five and I chuckle and then moan just a little bit, tangling my fingers in his hair. Finally he pulls away and picks up my right arm and lightly runs his fingers down my bicep as if marvelling over every little part of my body and then I hear a murmur of discontent.

"Aw, what's this scar?"

I pull my arm in, automatically self-conscious. I have a whole bunch of scars. They're so old that I often forget about them at this point. Nobody usually sees them. I've had my hook-ups with guys sure, but they usually didn't mean much and everything was done in the dark, the soft light of morning never laying me bare before somebody who really cared for me.

"That was my dad," I say. I know it's not my fault or

anything. But the scar is a thick white line that came from one of Didion's "tissue samples." It's not very pretty. "Please don't make a big deal out of it."

Xander doesn't say anything but he sits up a little, leaning on his elbow. He reaches over to caress my cheek. His gaze isn't pitying and I like that. Instead it's only steady and loving. "I had an anxiety attack last night," he says. Of all the things I might have expected Xander to say...this wouldn't be in the top thousand. "Yeah. A real anxiety attack. After that probation hearing... It didn't go great even though Jack is still locked up. It was kinda brutal. And then my dad read me the riot act. It was partly about you but that's not surprising. And my brother's pissed at me... And shit with the company... It was just too much shit at once and I had an anxiety attack."

"That sucks," I say. "How awful."

"It's okay, I don't need you to..." He licks his lips. I think it's hard for Xander to accept sympathy like that from anyone. "I used to get them all the time is the thing. When I was younger? I was so stressed out about being a perfect alpha and a perfect Tremblay and then a perfect CEO...I'd shake and my heart would race and I'd think I was having a heart attack. Honestly. I thought I was dying a whole bunch of times. A few times I forgot where I was or why I was there. Got terrible stomach cramps. But I just dealt with it myself. Never told a soul about it. Not even Mason. I haven't had one in a long time but I had one yesterday."

"You never told anyone?" I say, and I can't help but feel a little bit upset about that. It makes sense. I know how shifters are, wolf shifters in particular. He would've felt like it made him weak. But *still*. "Not anyone?"

"But I'm telling you," he says softly. He kisses the tip of my nose and smiles, adoring. "Because I know I don't have to hide from you." Ever so gently, he tugs on my arm and his fingers trace that scar again. "You don't have to hide from me either."

I feel winded. That wasn't what I was expecting and tears well up in my eyes. He leans forward and kisses each of my cheeks. "Thanks for being you," he says simply.

As much as we'd like to stay in bed all day, it's a work day and Xander just took the previous day off to go to that probation hearing. He looks bothered about work and basically anything that's not *us*. I can't help but think that this relationship is entirely responsible for making everything so hard and as if sensing my thoughts as he pulls on his trousers, having just dried off from the shower, he smiles over at me.

"You're the best thing in my life," he says. "I have a great life. Usually. And I don't mean things settle down, you won't be the best thing either. I mean...from now on you're the best thing."

I think I blush at that and he comes over to kiss me softly. "You bewitched me, witch," he says.

"Are you going to work like that?" I ask him. He's wearing what he came over in; trousers and a white t-shirt.

"I'll sneak in through the back," he says, winking. "I have suits at work."

"You keep extra suits at work?" I say, incredulous.

"Sure." He shrugs like everyone keeps extra suits at work. "Not because of mornings after like this either. But you never know what's going to happen and I spend so much time at the office..."

"It really wasn't for mornings after?" I say, disbelieving.

Xander looks just a little bit sheepish and says, "Not *usually*."

Xander's already running a little late but he insists on taking me along to work since I'm coming in for a few hours anyway. There's something so natural about it all. It doesn't feel at all strange that my boyfriend is the guy I was investigating for evil doings by his company. It feels like this is the way it's supposed to be. I'm his and he's mine. In the car, as he drives, he holds my hand and kisses my knuckles. He won't stop talking about my hair either. He can hardly keep his fingers out of it.

When he parks in the structure behind Tremblay Company though, he just sits there for a minute, staring. Sooner or later, I imagine things are going to catch up with him. As much as he might love me, I'm a human and he's a wolf and this has never been allowed. And for a Tremblay who's always followed the rules, I can't expect him to just forget his code.

"They're going to say I'm a traitor," he says softly.

I unbuckle my seatbelt but for a moment I just sit there with him, staring where he's staring. "I know. Do you think you are?"

"I am in *their* eyes," he mutters.

"What about in your own eyes?"

"The thing is, your own father was a shifter," he says, squinting. "So *how*... I mean you're not just some random human and even if you were, I'm getting to think that it shouldn't fucking matter. I know it would've mattered to me a few months ago."

And then I say what hurts to speak aloud but which I know is true. "If it comes down between me and everything else, you *can't* choose me, Xander. You know that, right?"

I fully expect him to agree albeit reluctantly because he knows how much it might hurt me to hear. But instead he just looks at me and gets out of the car without a word. I'm blown away. I can't count on that but I think it means he's not sure if he'd be able to choose *them* over me. And that's shocks me.

I get out of the car and watch Xander saunter through the

parking structure toward the backdoors of Tremblay Company. He turns his head to see if I'm following and then walks backwards, beckoning me because I guess I look reluctant but it's really because I'm so surprised. He's wearing those trousers and that thin white t-shirt and his hair isn't all styled neatly like it usually is. He looks about ten years younger as he grins at me, his laugh echoing in the garage.

I love that man.

I feel as if there are multiple Xander Tremblays I have yet to meet. And I can't wait to meet them all.

He gets a funny look from the receptionist in the lobby who's on the other end toward the front doors but she does see him making his way to the elevators with me having caught up. He's taken my hand in his, unapologetically and I bite my lip. I guess on the spectrum of things, the complication of dating a colleague is not his biggest problem but I've never worked in an office before this. I'm not sure how it'll go over.

Xander, however, seems to have no such concern as he smiles adoringly at me.

"Morning, Mr. Tremblay!" The receptionist calls out just as the elevator dings.

"Morning, Sally!" Xander and I step into the elevator and we don't make a clean get away as two other people (I don't know them) step inside with slightly raised eyebrows.

I guess I'll just have to get used to that.

But on the seventh floor, nobody looks twice, though we're not holding hands this time as we walk onto the floor. We part ways and Xander leaves me with a wink before sauntering into his massive office and I make my way all the way down to the other end of the floor to my much tinier office that still has a couple of boxes I haven't unpacked. I still have to ask IT to hook up my printer for me and the only reason I haven't is because I haven't needed to print anything. I *do* have my very favorite knicknack sitting on my desk however. It's a blue ceramic elephant. I like to think it brings me luck. It's a small office but I think it's cosy and anyway it still has a nice view. They actually offered me a larger one but considering I'm only here part-time to begin with, I felt like a jerk taking it and insisted on the smaller one.

Things with Chile are moving ahead. I have emails from diplomats and a few other corporate contacts who are showing solidarity, promising not to use any altanium mines in Chile at all until this is resolved. I handle a few emails and then head out to find the coffee cart that roams this floor around this time. There's also a regular old break room coffee but I feel like something fancy today.

I get myself a mocha and when I get back to my office, there's a rose on my desk and Post-It that just has a heart and a big X scribbled on it. It makes me smile and I sit back in my chair, smelling my rose and wondering how Xander managed to get one and have it sent to me so quickly. There's a half-full water glass on my desk and I drop the rose into it. I find myself all starry eyed and moony and when Xander happens to walk by my office, he looks over at me and I smile, probably looking like a completely love struck dope. Xander sees me and stops for just a second. He doesn't say a word. He just smirks and slips his hands in his pockets, nodding to himself before going on.

I have a feeling that I've unleashed a little something. It's another side of Xander. The sappy and romantic Xander. I'm very excited about seeing more of him.

Sadly though, that will have to wait. Because at around lunch time, Xander comes to my office. I see him through the window, making a beeline from across the floor, ignoring a couple people who are trying to talk to him. He's carrying his phone and he does not look happy at all as he stomps into my office and shuts the door. I was in the middle of writing a letter and now I stop, frozen and immediately filled with dread, as I watch panic play out across Xander's face. He runs a hand through his hair and stares at me with wide eyes.

"There's been a breakout at Mulligan," he says, breathing heavily.

"Mulligan," I mutter. "The shifter prison-"

"It's happened before," he says, shrugging. "Alice's brother got out but this… This was a mass breakout."

"Didion," I say, an icy feeling crawling up my spine.

"Yes," Xander whispers. "He's out."

It's the stupidest thing. I didn't know he was *in* until a couple days ago. As far as I knew, my father who basically kept me hostage and tortured me for years, was free as a bird since I ran away. And anyway, by then I was sure he was only glad to be rid of me. But I have always feared him. And now I'm dating his biggest enemy. If my father has it out for anyone, I'm guessing he has it out for Xander Tremblay.

"He escaped," Xander says again, plopping down in the chair across from me. "And a bunch of men from Hardwidge escaped too. Almost all of them, it looks like. Except for Alice's brother for some reason. I got a bunch of texts from Elroy Finch letting me know. Jason didn't even try to escape, that's strange…"

"Where do you think they'll go?" I ask. I wring my hands. Xander's going to need to deal with this. I know how he's considered a de facto leader in his clan. But I don't understand at all how he juggles it all, keeping this company he's built up so much going strong while remaining the most powerful voice among all the packs in the state. It's a crazy amount of responsibility he has. No wonder he used to have anxiety attacks.

Even now...he's not exactly looking calm. In fact, his breath seems short and his eyes seem glassy. I get to my feet quickly, shutting the blinds on my windows looking out on the floor so no curious onlooker can see the CEO having an anxiety attack in the middle of the day. Not that it should be anything to be ashamed of, despite how Xander has thought of it in the past, but people can be weird about that kind of thing. They might assume it's something to do with the company. My office came with a little office fridge and some Tremblay Company branded water. I pull a bottle out and slide it across the table.

"Breathe, Xander, "I say softly. "It's going to be okay. This is a problem...but we're going to get through it. Together. Nothing bad is happening right now."

"If he comes for you," Xander says, looking at me even as he trembles a little bit. "I'll protect you. Assuming I'm not flipping the fuck out. I've never panicked in a fight. I don't see why I'd start."

"I know, baby," I say, reaching over to squeeze his hand that rests on the table. "I know. I look after you, you look after me."

"Mates," Xander breathes.

"Mates."

CHAPTER ELEVEN: AARON

My mate is annoyed with me. Michelle thinks I was too hard on Xander. I *may* have been. He did come around in the end after all. But considering how much guff I and Micah have gotten due to our mate's histories and, well, *genetics*, I don't think I was out of line to be aggravated. If Michelle had turned out not to have the shifter gene at all, Xander would have raised hell at the idea of one of us marrying a straight up human.

I can't quite stop talking about this. Which is annoying Michelle because it's a pleasant Saturday morning and she wants to leave our problems at home for the day and have a nice time at the park with our pup, Trevor, who's just starting to walk. We're still getting ready for the morning. I have Trevor in my lap and I'm attempting to feed him some gross smelling sweet potato mush. He should be in his chair, but I love feeding Trevor, even now as he makes a mess of everything.

"I'm just saying," I grumble wiping sweet potato from my beard, as I bounce Trevor on my knee. "This cute human woman comes along and suddenly this all important code doesn't matter? I mean, I would've thought it would be *kind* of a problem for him."

"I'm sure it was," Michelle says, packing supplies into the baby bag. The park's got a petting zoo going on today. I've cleared space on my phone for pictures just for the occasion. I just hope he doesn't prematurely shift and try to kill a goat or something. Shifter kids don't usually start for a few more years yet but there are cases of pups shifting at a very early age.

It's not impossible. It's the perils of shifter kids.

"How are you not upset?" I say, throwing my hands up.

"Because he's your brother," Michelle says simply. "And I know that he would always have come around *just like he did*. And it's stupid to get so upset because he had a problem for five minutes-"

"It was longer than five minutes," I say darkly.

"Regardless," Michelle says, "he came around. And I think it would be wise of you to be the bigger man and support your brother now." She zips up the baby bag and raises her eyes at me. "Your father seems to think he's taking a human as a mate. Which...I do not understand this stuff at all, Aaron. If her father is a shifter, how is she human?"

"She can't shift," I say, shrugging.

"Yeah, well, neither can I."

"That's different."

"It really isn't," I mutter. "You all are basing these silly rules on some complicated genetics that you don't even understand, if you want to know my opinion. Anyway...I think you should support Xander. Because if this human woman is his mate...there's gonna be a lot of trouble. He's going to need you. And being petty about it isn't doing you any favors." She twists her mouth as she looks at me. It's that look she gets when I'm driving her to distraction. "Trust me, babe. It is *not* doing you any favors."

"Noted," I grumble."

Michelle signals she's not actually mad, kissing my neck as she brushes by me as I finish feeding Trevor, carefully wiping his mouth. I playfully bare my teeth and give him a little growl and he laughs, attempting to growl himself though it comes out more like a gurgle.

It takes another half an hour just to leave the house for a few hours in the park, though I know I'm going to be looking at my phone too often. The news came in last night via our shared text chat with Xander. There was a huge breakout at the shifter prison, Mulligan. We don't know what it means yet but it does make me sympathize with Xander a little. I know he has a lot on his plate right now. We're set to meet at the estate tonight too and discuss what comes next. I imagine that's going to be pretty awkward with everyone wondering what the state of Xander's relationship with this human witch person who is also, apparently, Jack Didion's *daughter*.

A tiny bit of paranoia in me wondered if this woman is still actually on Didion's side and if she has been preying on Xander from the beginning...but then why tell him she's his daughter... It didn't make any sense to me. But like I said, paranoid. Comes with being a wolf sometimes.

The drive to the park is short. Trevor's in a cheerful mood. He loves the park even though he's only old enough to go on the little toddler swings and we help him with the little kid house and some of the smaller jungle gym stuff, carefully helping him along. His favorite is the merry-go-round when one of us holds him and sit on it as the other gives it a gentle push. He seems to like the spin.

It's a beautiful day in the park. Trevor is impatient to try walking a lot now and we let him walk between us now and then, each of us holding a chubby little hand until he inevitably changes his mind and climbs back in the stroller.

When Michelle finally puts Trevor back in his stroller,

she rolls him over to look at the chickens, so I decide to take a minute and talk to Xander. I hate fighting with any of my brothers and for the most part, I feel that Xander and I have actually become much closer since I met Michelle. I don't want to stew about this when deep down, I know that Michelle is right in everything she said. Xander doesn't pick up. I imagine he's probably very busy, even on a Saturday. Instead of leaving a voicemail, I opt to text.

Hey X,

I'm a dick. Past is past. I know you'll always stand by me and I'll always stand by you. I'm sorry for being an asshole. Stay tuned for pics of Trevor + baby goats.

That should do it. But I still feel just a little bit tense even as I strode over to the chickens and see Trevor's eyes lighting up at all the strange new creatures he's seeing. But a minute later, my phone vibrates and it's Xander.

Nothing but love, bro. We're cool.

I know that's all I need to hear. If Xander were still pissed, he'd say so. I've been stewing on and off since I called him to yell at him, and now I feel much lighter, as if a few rough edges have been smoothed. I head over to Trevor and Michelle and we all lose track of time as we introduce him to baby goats and fluffy little lambs. The ice cream truck comes and we let him have some strawberry push pop before pushing him on the toddler swing. My phone is about dead but we don't feel like going home just yet so I kiss Michelle on the forehead and tell her I'm going to charge up in the car for a minute. We parked a couple blocks away, in sight of the park, and I set off at a trot. It's a little bit silly how desperate I love my mate and my pup. I don't want to miss a second of such a pleasant day out with them.

A block away from my SUV, I see a dark figure trotting away. It's a man wearing a hoodie and I wouldn't think much of it except that he smells like a wolf and that doesn't happen very often. He turns a corner and is gone quickly. Something about that bothers me but then again...paranoid. I sit in the driver's seat, intending to listen to the radio and charge up just enough to get me through a couple of hours until we go home. Michelle thinks I can be too addicted to my phone (that's a laugh considering her Instagram habits) but with everything going on, I like to be in contact.

When I turn the key in the ignition, I hear a funny noise. It's like an extra whirr and a click. It's pure instinct and nothing else that makes me grab my phone, jump out of the car, and run as my heart pounds.

A block away the explosion throws me forward and I hit the ground, falling into a crouch. When I roll over and sit up, I see my car has become a ball of flame as screams echo from the park just across the street. Whatever that was, it was considerable. The flames shoot up high as a couple people from the park run to help me to my feet and I'm stunned, my ears ringing, before I thank them but push them away and run for Michelle.

This is Jack Didion's work. I have no doubt.

This is a declaration of war.

CHAPTER TWELVE: XANDER

I'm at my place, having drinks with Olivia on my overpriced mid-century modern sofa in my too big, too fancy empty house when the news comes in. We were having a lovely day, despite everything including my father who I haven't spoken to since our fight. But my brother had just texted to smooth things over and I felt a lot better about that. Olivia had heard back personally from some shareholders who actually seem to *like* that we're heading in a distinctly more ethical direction. I hadn't heard anything good about finding our escaped convict shifters, but I wasn't too worried. But when my phone buzzes just as I'm pulling away from Olivia and smiling slyly as I reach for my wine, I realize that I should not have underestimated my enemies.

On the other hand, they should not be underestimating me either.

The text is from Michelle's phone and it says: Go to estate NOW 911 - X.

"I gotta go," I say immediately, practically shoving Olivia off my lap as I get to my feet. "Something happened and I don't know what, but it's gotta be bad. I have to go to my folks' house."

"Do you know what it is?" Olivia says, standing up, and I love how she just seems to know the score. That when something goes down, I'm the first phone call.

"No but we only use 911 if it's something big." I almost feel a rise of panic and Olivia turns me to face her and cups my cheeks in her palms. "You got this. Whatever it is. Okay?"

"Yeah," I mutter. "I know."

"Should I come with?"

I wince at that. It's not the right time. "Not yet," I say softly. "It's going to be a whole discussion. It'll be a distraction from whatever's happening. Stay here, would you? I have a good security system. I'd feel better about it. Place even came with a panic room, there's instructions-"

"I'm not going to use your panic room," Olivia says with a snort.

"The instructions," I say firmly, "are in the drawer by the phone in the kitchen. Just in case. Just give em' a look and humor me. I'll set the alarm on my way out. Eat whatever you want, place is fully stocked. Don't answer the door unless you know it's me."

"Well, I'm not a dumbass, Xander," she says, and kisses me once, sweetly. "It'll be okay."

"I'm...glad you believe that," I say, sighing.

When I get to the estate, everyone's car is already parked out front in the circular drive. I feel a chill in my bones. Something serious has happened. Everyone must have rushed right over, except that I don't see Aaron's SUV which immediately concerns me since I got the text from Michelle's phone. I feel a weird cold feeling in the tips of my fingers. I take a deep breath and manage to park without ramming anyone but I'm a little short of breath as I grab my keys and run to the door which my parent's butler opens before I even knock.

"In the parlor," he says, not quite looking at me. He looks pale as a ghost.

"What the hell happened?" I say, right on the verge of panic.

"Um...in the parlor, sir," he says uncertainly. "It's not my place-

"Xander!" My mother looks tearful and she runs to me even as I make my way to the parlor where everyone is gathered. "Somebody blew up Aaron's car! Oh my God!"

Aaron is dead.

I can't breath. My heart is in my throat. I feel panic rising inside me. I'm going to die, my heart is pounding so hard, my brother is dead...

"Aaron," I say, my voice cracking all over the place.

Tears rush to my eyes and I think my legs are about to give out beneath me. It's only my mother's weight on me, forcing me to support her that keeps me standing. When she pulls away, I think I will fall down. But then my brother walks out of the parlor to meet me. There is Aaron, looking mostly pissed. I feel as if all the blood is rushing down to my feet.

"Oh Jesus," I say tearfully. "I thought she meant... Jesus..." I rush to my brother and throw my arms around him, squeezing him as hard as I can. I've never felt a relief like this in my life. "Thought she meant you were dead, Aaron. Jesus *Christ*."

"Oh, I'm sorry!" My mother says, clapping a hand to her mouth. She waves a hand, making her way to the parlor. "I'm sorry, Xander. Aaron, I'll give you two a minute."

"I'm okay," Aaron whispers, embracing me. We let go and

he pats my shoulder. He looks fierce more than anything. I have to think nothing's happened to Michelle or Trevor or he wouldn't be this calm.

"Michelle and the pup?" I say, double-checking.

"Yeah, they're okay," he says firmly. "Everyone is here. Everyone is safe. I figured I should bring them here."

"What the hell is she talking about?" I say. I have to lean against the wall a little and catch my breath. "What's mom mean?"

"Went to the park with Michelle and Trev," Aaron says slowly. He looks exhausted. "We were there for a while. My phone was dead so I went to the car to charge it. I saw somebody running from near the car, wearing a hoodie, smelled like wolf but I didn't know the scent. Turned on the car and I heard a weird sound and...and I just had a *feeling* you know? So I took off running and just...boom." He shakes his head, his eyes as wide as saucers. "Car just went up like a goddamn... It was a big explosion, Xan. If Michelle and Trev had been in the car..."

I've been angry before. I've been *very* angry before. The only thing I have to compare *this* anger too is when Dax's men kidnapped Micah.

I'll kill them all.

I see red. That's the only way I can describe it. I'm so angry I feel dizzy.

"Didion," I whisper.

"That's what we all think." Aaron nods to the parlor and I follow him in where everyone is sitting around, drinking coffee and looking serious as they talk quietly. I know everyone is here before me only because Aaron and his family rushed here and I live the farthest away, but walking in like this while such an emergency is going on, I feel as if I've fucked up as alpha somehow.

119

But that's only a minor thought compared to the white hot heat of rage coursing through me.

All my brothers and their mates are here and my mother has a sleepy Trevor on her knee now, holding him tight.

I rub my eyes. "Didion must have teamed up with Dax's men from Hardwidge," I say. I pace around but everyone looks a little jittery so I sit in the big chair nearest Mason who's looking at me steadily. "They've declared war."

"That's what we're all assuming yeah," Mason says quietly.

"I'm gonna murder them." I almost laugh as I say it. "Just a second. I'll be back in a minute."

I spring up from my chair again and walk out of the room. I have too much enraged energy inside me and I don't have time to shift and I don't want to start screaming in that room with my mom holding Trevor on her knee, considering he saw a fucking explosion today. I can't imagine how that effected even a toddler. I go to the study and slam the door behind me and just stand there, breathing for a second.

"Xander." My father is sitting at his desk. He looks at me with those sympathetic eyes. I don't want to know what he wants to say. It was the same look he wore when he told me I was doing a shitty job with, well, *everything*.

"Just...not right now, dad." I pace around, he just watches and I end up facing the wall next to the big bookcase. I shut my eyes and all I see is red. I see myself tearing out Jack Didion's throat for very nearly murdering my brother and his mate and his child and for torturing my mate and for kidnapping Micah and his mate and I want to kill everyone who's helping him declare war on me and mine... I want it so badly I think I'll explode from the desire.

I scream right there. I scream out loud in my father's study like I'm a pissed off teenager again and after this I can pull it together but right now I have to scream. When I'm finally done I pull my fist back and the punch the wall.

120

"Son-"

"Don't," I say, sounding too young to my own ears. I don't sound like the strong alpha as much, I am not the strong alpha. I sound like the scared kid. I hate that. "Just don't right now," I say, my voice a bit steadier. "Okay?"

I feel better even though my knuckles are fucking killing me now. I take a breath and turn to face my father, massaging the back of my hand. There's no time for this bullshit. I know that. God knows what Didion and those Hardwidge bastards are planning and I know that Didion has allies who could help him. I have to move, I have to plan, I have to-

"I was wrong," my father says softly.

I feel a little bit like a teenager standing there about to get grounded. I'm wearing a t-shirt again. It's a Nirvana shirt of all things and some old jeans. Because when I got that text, Olivia and I were just lounging around at my place even as I occasionally worked and harangued Finch for more details about the breakout. Now I feel as if I was about to get grounded but have been granted a reprieve.

"Were you?" I say, crossing my arms and sniffing. I feel antsy. Nice as it is to hear my father say he was wrong about something. He stands from behind his desk and walks over to me. He's had a little bit of a limp for a long time and it seems more pronounced today. I wonder if the stress of what happened to Aaron has made him sore today and my heart squeezes a little in sympathy.

"I was," he says flatly. He takes a breath. He's wearing his reading glasses and now he takes them off, rubbing his eyes. "Things are changing in the clan. In all the clans, Xander. You must know that. It's not like it was. Old men like me, takes us some getting used to."

"What're you saying?" I ask him. He looks even more tired than Aaron does right now. And he looks old.

"I'm saying that you have always been true to the family and to the clan," my dad says slowly. "You are brilliant and yes, you can be hot-headed but that comes with the protectiveness that I know you feel towards those you love. You love with your whole heart and I know it's a big heart. But you're too loyal and too...*good* for me to think that whatever this is with this Olivia Hathaway, that it could possibly be wrong or a mistake."

"Are you serious?" I say, disbelieving.

"Xander...all this with Didion and Hardwidge...it's the ugly side of this...this *code* of ours. That's what I've come to realize. I feel sick about it now. That line of thinking is what almost killed Aaron. It's what tortured that poor girl and mistreated Alice and Luna. And that line of thinking has to die. Didion has declared war. But winning it won't just be about us beating him and his men. It will be about defeating these old, hateful ideas."

"And the company?" I ask him, expecting him to get stern again.

"The company is..." My father laughs and shakes his head. "Xander, what business have I to tell you how to head that company anyway? You're the one who's made it the leader in aerospace that it is today. You've made it into a multi-billion dollar corporation. You should have told me off for what I said to you."

I snort at that and just look at him. He's about four inches shorter than me but he has always loomed large.

"You're my father," I say simply.

He smiles at that and nods and then he hugs me, and we embrace, firmly, patting each other on the back. I don't know what's ahead. But I feel a little better about things now with things repaired between me and my family. All this time I've been thinking that all this was on my shoulders as the alpha. But in truth, I couldn't do any of this without their support and their belief in me. It's never been just my strength that's kept me going all these years even as the responsibilities piled on top of me one after the other. It's been them helping to hold me up.

"Just tell me one thing before we go in there," he says, nodding toward the parlor. "Do you truly resent taking over the company?" He shakes his head, looking bemused and I feel a bit mortified. In my most stressed out and darkest moments I do feel resentment that I wasn't so much given a choice as to whether I'd take over the family business. It was absolutely expected of me.

"Oh... Um." I sigh and scratch my head, wincing. "Sometimes I do. Other times I love it. It's just one of those things. But I don't...I'm not bitter about it or anything."

"We should talk about that," my father says, still looking bothered.

"Yeah, well..." I nod at the door. "Sometime maybe. Right now, I got a war to fight."

"Alright," he says, squeezing the back of my neck. "But this conversation isn't over."

"If you say so," I say, chortling despite myself.

First things first, we need to know who our allies are because I need to hold a meeting of all my alphas and elders but I'm not about to invite over *everyone* since I'm absolutely sure that not everyone is on my side. My father and I return to the parlor and my brothers and I start making calls, feeling people out. A lot of it is instinct. We start with our known, deepest, oldest allies and ask them what they know. I already know some people I can definitely skip. I'm not even going to bother calling anyone who voted for Didion to be released from Mulligan and that's a whole bunch of people. A few people call me before I get a chance to call them, quickly hearing about the explosion through the grapevine once we start making phone calls. It doesn't take long. But it feels good to get those calls from the diehard who swear their fealty even if it means they'll have to fight against people they've casually socialized with. A few of the biggest packs are definitely on my side. That's good. It brings the numbers up if there's a real fight.

I can't help but think that at some point, Didion is going to make an attack on the estate. I just don't see it *not* happening. He's trying to take us down. That much is clear.

After a lot of phone calls and long conversation and way too much coffee, we all break for dinner. Dinner is some kind of wine beef stew tonight and at first I have to make myself eat it but soon enough I'm scarfing down thirds. Weirdly, I'm feeling pretty good. I think it's the wolf in me; the true alpha. I'm comfortable with a fight. At least fights are clear cut. You're on my side or you're not. Protect the pack and anyone who tries to hurt it is the enemy. It's not complicated and it tells me at whom I am baring my teeth.

In between, I find a few times to text Olivia to make sure she knows I'm safe. I feel conflicted about her being there alone in my house now. It's safe, sure. But I don't like thinking of her as separate from the family. We both know she's my mate now. It's beyond any doubt. That means she's family and she should be here.

"Invite her," Mason says, nudging me at the dining room table. We've all got our phones out even as we try to eat and talk to each other all at the same time. The women too look as fired up as anyone else and I see Luna looking especially pissed off. I wouldn't want to tangle with her if I was Didion or one of his men, that's for sure.

"Mason..." I frown at my phone. "I have to stay here but... Do you think you could go pick up Olivia for me?"

"Yeah?" Mason says. It's nearly eight now. It's just barely dark but there's no way I'm letting any of us travel alone right now, especially when Olivia can't shift. "I think that's a good idea. She should be here."

～

"We all know why we're here," I say later, standing in front of the gathering of elders and alphas all crowded into my father's study. My father is here too, standing right beside me with my brothers. He's an elder but he hasn't been involved much in pack or clan decisions for a while. I took it as him leaving me to take the lead without the intimidation of his shadow and I always appreciated that part of it. But now is a time to show Tremblay solidarity and I only feel stronger with him and my mother at my side with my brothers. Olivia is here too, though she's sitting in the back of the room because I don't want to make it obvious who she is or have anyone bother her. Honestly, I didn't want her at this meeting at all for her own sake, but she insisted.

"We're here," I say, my voice thundering under the vaulted ceiling of the library, "because a once vaunted alpha of this clan has declared war on my family, my pack, and depending on the loyalty of all who gather here, on this clan. This afternoon, there was an attempt made on the life of my brother, his mate, and their young pup..."

Everyone's eyes turn to Aaron and then to Michelle and Trevor sitting on a chaise near him. Michelle looks stoic and I see Aaron reach over to squeeze her hand.

"They used a powerful explosive to blow up his car," I say, my voice shaking with anger. "The only reason my brother isn't dead right now, is sheer instinct and dumb luck. What I need to know first, before anything else is said, is if anyone here knows *anything* about who Jack Didion might be working with or who he has allied himself with. If any of you have information, stand up *now*."

I cross my arms, looming over all the alphas and elders sitting there in the folding chairs the butler set out for them and eating the cheese and crackers that my mother put out with tea because God forbid even a war meeting occur without refreshment.

A young alpha I don't know very well named Griffin from Bellingham gets to his feet and says, "I know something."

The kid can't be more than twenty. He's got to be a pretty green alpha and Bellingham is so far up north, I can't think it's got much to do with Didion but that doesn't mean he might not know somebody who knows somebody and I give him a nod. "Alfred Griffin," I say, for all to hear, "tell us what you know then?"

The kid looks petrified but there is a fire in his eyes and he says, "*I* know what everyone here knows. Which is that the most powerful leader in our clan, Xander Tremblay, is mated to a human woman, Olivia Hathaway, supposed daughter of Jack Didion-"

There's an eruption of shouts and gasps and grumbles at that and rage courses through me, especially when I catch Olivia's gaze across the room and see her looking so troubled.

"She is not the supposed daughter of Jack Didion," I say, clenching my fists to stop myself shifting and mauling the boy until I feel better. "She is the *actual* daughter of Jack Didion. Anyone who knows the details of Didion's attempt to gain probation, knows that he did not deny keeping his daughter hostage and experimenting on her in the name of breeding shifters, torturing her for years and holding her against her will..." I see Olivia is about to cry and I stop, taking a breath. Going over and over that can only upset her more. "She is human, yes. And..."

Everyone is staring at me. I suddenly feel the weight of generations of expectation on my shoulders but I also feel my love for my mate tugging at me. I feel as if I'm being pulled in two directions, as if all of this will tear me apart until there is nothing left.

"And if the fact of Olivia Hathaway being human is enough to make you forget that Jack Didion attacked my sister-in-law and just attempted to kill my brother and her and their son, then you don't belong here and I'll be happy to see you go. And if I meet you on the field of battle, I will not forget the choice you've given me."

There's a kind of hush that falls over the whole room, not just because I've made a potential threat but also because I haven't confirmed or denied that Olivia is my mate.

An elder named Santino from Spokane stands. Elders are always a lot more diplomatic and this one is smiling kindly before he speaks, everyone quieting so he can be heard.

"Xander," Santino says slowly, "do we know conclusively that this was Didion's work?"

"We don't," I say, inwardly calming myself. It's a totally fair question. I have no proof at all as obvious as it all seems. "The timing would strongly suggest it, given Didion's history with my family and that I've just testified against him. I'm sure you all know that he's reported to have broken out of Mulligan as well, along with several men from the Hard-widge pack in Oregon. Obviously that pack also has a vendetta against my family. All this would seem to suggest an alliance between them."

"I agree with you," Santino says, looking me in the eye. "I also don't believe that Xander Tremblay who has been an accomplished and stalwart alpha for nearly twenty years, needs to prove his loyalty to this clan for us to stand behind him. Xander, would you move to put us on a war footing right now?"

I take a deep breath. Everything in me wants to say "yes" but I know how alphas can be. We're all a bit hot-headed.

127

The ones who *might* have a problem with me but can be won over to fight a war need to be eased in. I glance at my father and his steady gaze gives me an answer. Wisdom is more important than strength, he used to tell me. That's why we have elders in the first place.

"I think we need to return to our packs," I say slowly, "and prepare to be on a war footing. Circle the wagons, gather our foot soldiers... I imagine if there is a target, it is this estate but if you are a close friend or ally of my family, you might send your pups and those who cannot fight somewhere safe for the time being."

"Shall we take that to a vote?" Santino says.

Everyone agrees to vote and the decision passes. This basically means, I'm going to need to send my brothers out and find out in private who is with me and who isn't. No one but an angry little green alpha like Alfred Griffin is going to put himself out there and risk being mauled on the spot.

When the meeting is over though, and they all start to leave, even after more than half of them waiting to speak to me and pledge their loyalty, I don't feel much better. Olivia finds me when they're all gone and kisses me and tells me I did great and when I thank her, I feel like a complete asshole. I didn't stand up for her. I didn't stand up for my mate. Yet I don't know how I would have done so with centuries of expectation on my head.

I wonder if, by the time this is over, I'll really have been torn in two.

CHAPTER THIRTEEN: OLIVIA

"**I** can't believe I'm at work," Xander says, giving me an aggrieved look as we ride up in the elevator on Monday.

"Yeah, I was wondering what you were doing here," I say, leaning against him a little. "Thought you'd be at the estate, ya know...plotting."

"Strategizing," Xander says.

"Fine, strategizing." I roll my eyes but I can't help worrying. A lot. About all of this craziness. "This is my first shifter war. Don't know all the correct terminology." I shift on my feet and run a hand through my mass of curls. Since we're blessedly alone in the elevator and nearly to the seventh floor, Xander takes advantage and slips an arm around my shoulders, kissing me on the cheek. I'm wearing trouser jeans and a black t-shirt with a colorful sweater today. It's my compromise on work wear since Xander seems upset somehow that I wasn't dressing like myself. I guess I need all the breaks I can get to concentrate on work today. I can't imagine how Xander is handling it.

"My brothers convinced me come in," Xander says, sighing. "They think I'll go nuts if I sit at the estate waiting to either make a move or for Didion to make another one."

"Why don't you make a move then?" I say, raising an eyebrow.

"Well," he says with a snort, "for one thing, I don't know *where* they are. I'm also not entirely sure who they all are. My instinct is to attack first and ask questions later. That worked for saving Mica and Luna. It's not going to work for this war."

"Sounds wise," I say, returning his kiss on the cheek. I pull away quickly as the doors open and we step out onto the floor. I'm still worried though. Xander has too much on his plate on a *good* day and Tremblay Company is a little precarious right now. "Are you going to be alright?"

Xander avoids my eyes but he shrugs and puts on his what is obviously a pretence of nonchalance. "Sure thing. Call you if I need you."

"Do that," I say sternly, so he knows I'm not joking. He nods at that and heads to his office and I watch him go. I have a feeling he's not nearly as fine as he's acting.

Before lunch, I get a memo from Xander going out to everyone in the company including the shareholders and board that the Godrun drone has been not just suspended but that all future manufacturing of it is cancelled. Something about it seems too alarming and I suck in a breath. The shareholders were already panicked enough about the suspension but he'd suggested that once they were able to work something out with a more ethically run altanium distributor or if they figured how to build it with a different metal, the drone would be manufactured and sold.

This would suggest something completely different. The Godrun drone design is so stealthy and potentially lethal, that I didn't want it made at all and one glance online shows that lots of people who know about it don't, including *some* shareholders. But to cancel it so abruptly via *email...*

Something isn't right.

I jump up from my desk and everyone else on the office floor is looking slightly panicked and glancing towards Xander's office which has the door shut and the blinds drawn.

I knock on the door and say, "Xander, it's me." It takes a minute but the door opens a crack and I slip inside, shutting it behind me.

Xander looks like a mess. He's clearly had some kind of freak out since I left him at the elevator that morning. His eyes are wide and rimmed red and his hair is a mess like he's been tugging at it. He turns away from me and sits behind his desk, swivelling around to look out the window.

"It was wrong," he says quietly. "You were right. It was wrong. It's wrong...*I'm wrong.*"

I take a deep breath and sit across from him. He's muted his desk phone but I can see every single line lit up like Christmas as his cell vibrates like crazy on his desk. I can see email after email appearing in his Outlook on his computer screen.

"Did you have a panic attack?" I ask calmly.

He nods once and says nothing.

"I'm a fighter," Xander says quietly. He won't look at me while he speaks. He's staring out the window at his sprawling view of Quinton. "But I hate war. Always have. It's because I remember when I was a boy and my father had to go fight to defend some territory from some other clan... I was always so afraid for him. My mother was strong but she was afraid for him too. I was expected to be strong for my brothers...as the future alpha. But every time he had to go fight, I was afraid he wouldn't come back. And sometimes it was one of his friends who wouldn't come back but he did and I was happy. I hated being happy that someone else had been killed. I hated being happy that some other pup had just lost his father. Yet I love to fight, I love the rush of it. But I hate war. Both these things are true."

"Xander-"

"You said the Godrun drone would be used for war," Xander says, turning in his chair now to face me. "Not by us, of course, but by humans. Their wars are bigger...which is a bit like saying the sun is big compared to earth. When *we* fight...civilians don't die often. Innocent pups don't die often. Humans are rarely so careful."

"You're panicked about this war with my father," I say quietly. "It made you panic about the drone."

"You said I shouldn't make the drone too!" Xander sputters.

"Yes," I say, "and I'm glad you've changed your mind, but the....way you've done this-"

He seems to suddenly realize the extent of what he did; cancelling the biggest project of a company worth billions with one brief email and no explanation. He rubs his chin, his eyes wide and worried. "Yeah..."

"You can't do all this by yourself," I say slowly.

He jumps to his feet and says, "I gotta go."

"What? Xander!"

"I gotta go," he says. "I gotta go home."

"*Now?*" I ask him. "After that memo?"

"Do you really think that matters?" He says, stepping in close to me and getting in my face. "Do you think that *any* of this matters? Compared to my family? To their lives? To the lives of the clan?"

There's a knock at the door and Xander barks, "What?"

The door isn't locked and Ryan from down in HR pokes his head in. He's the guy who handled my on-boarding and he's looking at Xander like he's afraid he might collapse at some point. "Hey, Mr. Tremblay. May I come in?"

Xander nods curtly and Ryan walks in, holding a binder under his arm. I see two security guards standing just outside and it makes the hair on my neck stand up.

"Ah, some member of the board have spoken to me," Ryan says slowly. "They're rather concerned about this memo..."

"I'm the CEO," Xander growls.

"Yes," Ryan says. "No doubt about that. But uh...well, they are just concerned about your state of mind and they would like you maybe to go home for a few days." He smiles as if he's just given Xander great news. It almost makes me laugh. "Just go home, relax a little bit. Maybe see a doctor? Get a clean bill of health? And the rest of us will handle things while you take a little break."

That sounds alarmingly like he's about to get ousted and I look to Xander, expecting him to toss out some obscenities and slam the door in his face.

Instead Xander says, "You know what? Sounds good." He grabs his jacket. "I'll see you in a few days."

"Oh..." Ryan looks as shocked as I am. "Didn't expect that to actually work."

"Me neither," I say and all I can do is stare when he pecks a kiss to my forehead before walking out the door.

Ryan gives me a funny look and says, "Are...are you two officially involved?"

"Is that really at issue right now?" I say, about to blow my own top.

Ryan looks a bit sheepish at that and nods. "Eh, we'll talk about it later. Do you mind locking up his office?"

"Sure," I say, shrugging.

This is bad, I think to myself. This is all very bad.

❧

For the rest of the day, I find myself putting out small fires as much as I can. It doesn't even make sense. I'm not even assistant to the CEO. My job is in one subset of PR, yet everyone has caught on to the fact that I'm close to Xander and they assume I know what he's thinking or doing at any given time. I find myself fielding a lot of phone calls and emails and assuring them that Xander Tremblay knows exactly what he's doing and that their patience is appreciated. After an hour of that, I actually go to my car and grab some emergency spell ingredients and whip up a brew for calmed states and financial stability. I'm hoping that if nothing else, the stock will stop dropping. It was only just recovering from the initial drop after the suspension of the drone but now I'm seeing it take a nosedive when I check it on my phone.

I hate worrying about things like stocks but here we are.

Things do calm down a little bit and if I do say so myself, sometimes I forget what a good witch I am. But a spell like that is really only a short term solution.

The problem is that Xander can't handle pack and clan business right now and run his company at the same time, if he ever could. But I don't know if he'll be willing to admit that.

On the other hand, he just panicked and bolted. So maybe he'll be willing to listen for a half a minute.

Work at the Tremblay Company keeps me so busy, I hardly know how fast the day is passing until I get a text from Mason Tremblay saying that Xander is home and not answering his phone and everyone is worried. I reflexively text back that I'm wrapping up and I'll go talk to him.

I can't imagine I'm going to be more persuasive than Xander's own brother and oldest confidante, but if Mason thinks I will be, I'm willing to try.

~

It's after nine by the time I finally leave the office and get over to Xander's house. I guess the good news is that my father hasn't made another move yet. He seems to be biding his time. Or else he's plotting an attack.

Hopefully, it will be enough time for the clan's most powerful alpha to get his shit together like I know he can.

I take a deep breath when I reach the door but he opens it before I can ring the doorbell or knock.

"You shouldn't be here," Xander says darkly, glaring at me before he pulls me inside, looking over my shoulder outside as he shuts the door. "You shouldn't have come here alone. What if one of Didion's people had seen you?"

"I can take care of myself," I say, glaring right back.

Xander's wearing jeans and no shirt and he's holding a bottle of whisky. He's got dark circles under his eyes. I suppose he did when he came in this morning. I wish I'd noticed before. I sigh and stand on my tip toes, reaching up to stroke his cheek. "Baby," I murmur. "I'm worried about you."

"I'm fine," he murmurs, ducking his head even as he leans into the touch. He takes a swig of whiskey and sits on his couch, sinking his head in his hands as he sets the bottle down. Nothing about this scene exactly screams "fine."

"You need to talk to me," I tell him, sitting on the table across from him. "Or talk to somebody. You're trying to handle this all on your own and it's freaking you out so badly, you can't handle *anything*. And I know you're stronger than that."

"If I'm so strong, what am I doing here hiding from my company and my pack and my clan with a bottle of whiskey," Xander says, slurring just a little. He rubs his eyes and I take a breath and the bottle, setting it on the table and out of his reach. "Listen to me," I say slowly. "You have been doing *everything* for your people, for your family, for the board and the shareholders... You have been carrying this for *years.*" I take his hands in mine and wait until he raises his eyes to meet mine. "It was too much for anyone and you carried it. Your dad may have founded that company but you've made it what it is. You've made your pack and your clan what it is today. Things are changing. You know that now. You've had to face it. Your clan is going to be a leader in how packs act after what happened with Hardwidge. And you are leading that clan. Xander..." I cup his cheek again, and find myself overwhelmed with love for him. "You're so good at leading. You just need to know when to let other people *help* you. You can't do this all on your own anymore. And part of that is because of how you've changed it all. Let people help you."

I can tell he's listening. He's looking at me steadily and I see him absorbing what I say. Even though we started out at odds, I feel like we understand each other in a way I've never understood or been understood by anyone.

"I should've stood up for you," Xander says, reaching up to clasp my hand against his cheek. "I could have told them all that you *are* my mate because you are," he says fiercely. "And I just...let it lie. Feel like I betrayed you."

"I didn't expect you to do that," I say softly, though I'm touched that he's bothered by it. "Xander, you forget. I grew up with shifters. I know how it goes. I may have been trapped in that lab for most of my childhood but I got a really good idea of how it works. And I've known shifters since then. No human mates. I didn't expect you to blow that up suddenly."

"I want to," Xander says, his eyes now looking a little brighter as he sits up a little straighter. "I want to stand up in front of them all and tell them that you are mine and I am yours. Because the rules need to be rewritten, Olivia." He laughs to himself, shaking his head. "That's what I've learned. It all started with Aaron falling for Michelle and the clan having to accept a mate with a shifter gene. You're right. Things are changing. How we deal with humans and how we live as packs and what code we follow... It's all changing. I can't help but think it's going to be a new age for shifters."

The way he's talking, his eyes so bright and clear and intense, he's giving me tingles. I can see why people follow him and trust him. He makes you want to trust him to lead.

"And if that's true... The clan's going to need an alpha who can guide them through the new age. And right now they need an alpha to be a general of war."

Xander takes a deep breath and gets to his feet. I watch him walk over to the windows that look out over Quinton. He sticks his hands in his pockets. I can practically hear the machinery of his mind whirring.

"I think I need to ask Mason to step in as CEO," Xander says.

"Oh!" I say in surprise. "I wasn't expecting that."

"Yeah..." He spins around and runs a hand through his hair. "Not the first time I've thought of it actually. He is on the company payroll since he does so much money and investment stuff for us. But I've...I've run everything by him since the beginning. We don't always agree but he always has good ideas and... I don't know who else I'd trust for that job other than my dad. And it's time...for me to not have that job. At least for a while."

"Are you sure?" I ask him. "You're going to step down? You're absolutely sure?"

"Olivia," Xander says, rolling his eyes. "What have we just been talking about? You're right about everything and I'm right too. It's a new day for shifters and being the leader the clan needs right now is way too much to juggle with being CEO of the company. It's not like it's the first time I've thought of that, it's just...hard to admit I can't actually do *everything*."

"Do you think Mason would agree to that?"

"Yes," Xander says, without hesitation. "If I tell him I need him, which I clearly do… he'll be there for me. He always is." He smiles fondly and says, "All of them always are."

"So... the plan is to put Mason in charge of the company," I say slowly. "And then you can concentrate on the war and whatever comes next." I step up in front of him and he slides his hands around my waist and nods.

"And I'll have Aaron and Micah by my side for the strategy," he says. "Aaron's good at that sort of thing. You know, if I wasn't alpha, I'd want him to be."

"Have you told him that?" I say, a little taken aback.

"I have," he says smiling.

"What a good brother you are."

He titters at that but his smile turns serious as he takes a long look at me and pushes a bright red curl behind my ear. "I don't know how I got so lucky as to meet you," he says, looking a little awestruck. "You understand me so well. You get it. All of it. I wouldn't want to change a thing about you. Nothing. I wouldn't want you to be a shifter just to make life easier or any shit like that. I love everything about you just as you are now."

I'm a little winded at that, especially under the intensity of his gaze and I suck in a breath. "You really know what to say to a girl, Xander Tremblay." I rest my forehead against his and we stand like that for a bit, just swaying there together, basking in the light of the bond between us that I know can never be broken no matter how much anyone might try to shatter it.

"Next time," Xander whispers in my ear, "I stand up for my mate."

CHAPTER FOURTEEN: XANDER

I've thought about having a mate before. I've thought about having a mate plenty of times. I guess I didn't have very specific expectations for it other than wanting it so badly in a vague kind of way. I've always wanted somebody *there* who I would wake up with in the morning. But I never really thought about having a mate who would understand me so completely. I suppose I always thought a mate would obviously understand shifter life, having always assumed I would end up with a shifter. But beyond that, I pictured a mate wouldn't understand what it is to be an alpha and a Tremblay and the defacto leader of a whole clan. Even my brothers don't completely understand it sometimes. In a way, they're actually too close to see it all steadily.

And then this human comes along...

If I ever doubted that Olivia is my mate, I can't now without lying to myself. She might be human but she gets me like no one ever has. She sees how I'm constantly forced to make impossible choices; between company and family, between clan and pack... She can see my strengths and weaknesses so clearly, it almost makes me uncomfortable yet I know it's good for me.

"I'm going to send Micah and Aaron out," I say now as I throw on a fresh shirt. Olivia has her phone out. She's texting my brothers a couple updates as she shifts from foot to foot. "They can round up our definitive allies."

"Hey...oh!" Olivia gasps a little and says, "Aaron says your dads has heard from Lou Sherman? From Olympia? His son ran into one of the Hardwidge boys who got loose lipped talking about taking on the Tremblays... His son played along, trying to get some information... Said they're going to attack the estate."

I stop abruptly with a jerk and take a breath, sliding my arms into the sleeves before buttoning up. I'm not surprised exactly. I fully expected that eventually there would be an attack on the estate. And yet, it's a shock to hear it stated as a fact. It's a shock too to fully absorb how much a bunch of people want me and my family dead.

"Do they know when?" I ask her, turning around. She looks horror stricken as she stares down at the phone. I watch her swallow and I watch her little porcelain face shift, the line of her mouth firming up. It's like I can see her physically trying to accustom herself to the notion of a war.

"Soon, they think," Olivia says softly.

"Right." I nod but no panic sets in. I feel much calmer now. I have a plan and I know what's coming. It's just a matter of being prepared for it. "So we'll...have to do this quickly."

"You still going to appoint Mason as CEO?" Olivia says.

"Yeah," I say, grabbing my jacket. "Too many rely on the company. I can't appoint second best. They deserve better. So... Micah and Aaron will go out to round up the allies. Send foot soldiers. We'll have to secure the estate. Put a guard all around the forest. God, we're gonna need a hundred guards for that."

"Should I be taking notes?" Olivia says.

"No," I say with a snort. I put on my jacket and turn around to see Olivia pocketing her phone, breathing deep, and looking a lot more nervous than I am now. But she stands up straight, looking at me steadily. *My mate.* "You're not my secretary. Besides...I'll remember."

I check myself in my closet mirror. Lately I've been looking older and more haggard than I feel but now as I see myself, I look not exactly young. I wouldn't quite feel right if I looked very young. But I look good and I look strong. I look like an alpha leading a war.

"Gorgeous," Olivia says, appearing by my side and turning my head to kiss me.

"You talking to yourself?" I murmur against her mouth before giving her another peck. She giggles into my neck and I can't imagine that I'll ever stop feeling my heart swell at the sound.

We allow ourselves just one minute of canoodling and then I pull away and take Olivia's hand in mind as we head to the front door.

"You ready for this?" I say, glancing back at her.

"Not in the slightest," she says, laughing. "Glad you are though."

"Yeah," I say, leading her out the door and shutting it behind me. "I'm ready."

~

"Me?" Mason says, his eyes uncharacteristically wide. I don't often see Mason looking surprised but now he sure does.

We're all gathered in the study again. Tremblay family only, this time. That means me, my parents, my brothers, their mates, and Olivia. I could kill for a little more of that whiskey to take the edge off of things but I'm resisting. I'd be better to stay stone cold sober and keep my wits about me.

"You...you want me to be CEO?" Mason says. "Am I hearing you right?"

I talked to my dad first when we arrived at the estate. I don't technically need his approval, but I was relieved to get it. I was surprised by how much he supported the idea. Apparently my mother's been yelling at him because she thinks he's responsible for putting too much weight on my shoulders. Yet as much as I read him the riot act not long ago, I don't blame my father for what I do as an adult. I've made my choices. And my dad seems to have taught me well enough that I don't regret many of them. Though admitting I couldn't do it all myself seems to have been the hardest lesson to learn.

"I think it's the right choice," my father says now from his seat on the chaise next to my mother. "For what it's worth."

"I didn't expect this," Mason mutters. He doesn't look bothered at least, just a little winded. I know he didn't expect to be running the company at all. But it's not necessarily forever either. I see him exchanging a look with Alice beside him that I can't read. That's been another thing to get used to. My brothers and their mates all seem to have these secret little communications between them. I suppose I'll have that with Olivia soon enough.

"Listen, Mason," I say, sighing. "I'm not gonna make you take it on if it's something you really don't want to do."

"It's not that," Mason says quickly. "I'm up for the challenge, I think it might be...interesting. Just surprised you're asking me," he says, chuckling. "But if you need me, I'm there."

"I definitely need you."

"Then I'm there," he says, shrugging as if it's no big deal

taking over a multi-billion dollar aerospace company. I have complete faith in him though. He's been there since the beginning. He's also well liked by the shareholders which is a huge factor. I think he's going to help even things out after this chaotic period.

"Then we'll announce it tomorrow at the board meeting," I say, plopping down in the chair behind my father's desk. I point to Aaron and Micah. "Next, I need you two to make the rounds and find out who's really on our side. We need foot soldiers and we need them now. A defence of the estate all around the woods and in front. And they need to get here in the next three days, the sooner the better."

Aaron exchanged a look with Micah and says, "We'll leave tonight."

"Going to need someone to clean up in the woods," I say, rubbing my eyes. "There are too many places for enemies to hide out there..."

"We can work on that," Luna says. She looks to Michelle, Alice, and Olivia who's standing uncertainly off to the side. "Write a list. We'll handle securing the estate. I have to think our resident witch here has some tricks up her sleeve." She smiles warmly at Olivia and I feel so grateful I have to stifle the sappy smile creeping up on my face.

"I absolutely do," Olivia says, giving her a wink.

"I'll do what I always do," my mother says. She's leaning against a bookcase with Trevor in her arms, swaying side to side. "Feed your army."

"Thanks, mom," I say. As if hearing her, my stomach grumbles but I don't think anyone heard it. The one thing I've forgotten to do today is eat. Can't forget those simple things. Besides which, I'm a nightmare when my blood sugar is low.

"What about battle strategies?" Aaron says. "I mean I can help you when I get back with Micah and Mason when he's

ABIGAIL RAINES

not at work but you should have something set in stone sooner rather than later."

I smile at my dad and say, "That's what the old man here is for."

Everyone looks sort of surprised by that, as little as my dad has been involved. But I'd be a fool not to take advantage of his knowledge. He's fought in plenty of battles himself even if they were a long time ago.

"So first things will be Mason taking over," I say, sighing. "Get that in line... But also..."

I glance over at Olivia. She tilts her head, looking at me in question. Her riot of red hair is tied back now and her face is so open as she blinks at me, waiting patiently for whatever's next. My lovely mate.

"Olivia is my mate," I say simply, my eyes still on her. Everyone titters slightly but I don't hear a shocked gasp. I guess everybody saw this coming. "I regret not confirming that the other day, but it's true. I have no doubt in mind. And I know she's human and that this flies in the face of..." I shake my head. "*Centuries* of this code of ours but... I know what the fates are telling me and she knows too..."

"I do," Olivia says softly, and it sounds so much like a wedding vow, I shiver.

"I need to know if any of you are going to have a problem with that," I say carefully.

"No, son," my father says, sighing. "We've talked about it. A *lot*. But I think we all know, from what we've seen and heard, Olivia is the woman for you." My father actually smiles at Olivia and that does make me gasp just a little. "The *mate* for you. It's surprising, yes. But given all the surprises this family has met with when my sons found their mates..." He grins at everyone and everyone kind of chuckles and looks pleased if put on the spot. "This does feel...like fate. And fate is a funny thing. But we won't stand in your way,

144

son." He nods to Olivia and says, "Welcome to the Tremblays."

I feel so relieved at those words, I'm dizzy with it and Olivia's eyes are watery when I look at her. But I only nod firmly before I go on.

"Things are changing," I say sternly, looking around at my brothers and their mates. "You all knew that before I did. Michelle, Luna, Alice... You've all been catalysts for a new age of what it means to be a shifter and be in a pack and have a mate. This *war*, this battle...it's about who gets to decide how we change and how we grow. What the future will look like. I know what the vision of Didion and Hardwidge looks like. It's ugly, brutal, prejudice. I want *your* vision," I say, looking at the women who have changed my family's lives. "I want your vision to become our vision. That's our fight."

"That's wonderful to hear from you, Xander, "Alice says, beaming up at me. Of any of us, I believe she's the one most driven to inspire changes for shifters and I think they're positive changes. Some of the alphas and elders have been resistant but that only means I need to support her cause in writing new rules for how mates and pups are treated within packs. The old fashioned types think that's some kind of infringement on their freedom. But people like Alice know, it's an expansion of *their* freedom.

"This isn't going to be easy," I say, laughing. "Because none of this ends with this war. It's going to go on and sometimes it's going to be messy but it's the future we're securing for not just this family but all the other pack's families. And...I'm grateful that I have you all beside me to help me fight for it."

By the time I'm done with my little speech, everyone's near tears and my mother insists on a round of hugs that don't seem very war-like but which we probably all need.

There's no time to waste really. We need to swing into

action. Micah and Aaron need to go start making their rounds to people and Mason and I need to call a meeting of the board.

"Nobody's going anywhere," my mother says, smirking, when I imply that everything needs to begin right exactly now. "Not until you all get some food in your stomachs. Don't think I missed that stomach grumble, Xander Tremblay."

I turn red at that and I hear Olivia chuckle behind me before my mother floats over to her and takes her arm. "And you, my dear, what's your favorite thing for dinner? We're always taking requests. *Also*, you haven't seen the rose garden!"

"Mom!" I say, throwing up my hands. "We don't have time for the rose garden. We're at war!"

CHAPTER FIFTEEN: OLIVIA

I 've made magical wards before. They're sort of like magical, invisible force fields. They can't completely repel anybody but they can repulse. They're mainly for a medium level of protection of a house and if your enemy has a decent warlock or witch they'll sniff it out quickly even if it takes them a while to break it. The advantage is in the other side having to break it. That can take anywhere from twenty minutes to six hours depending on the strength of the ward and the strength of enemy. And that precious time can be spent plotting the defence or offense.

I'm surprised and pleased to discover there's not much awkwardness in getting to know Michelle and Luna and Alice. They're all so welcoming.

"I've been exactly where you've been," Michelle says, laughing as she takes my arm. "We all have. This place can be so intimidating." Alice and Luna glance at each other and start laughing because, I suppose, they're all in agreement.

"I mean, we're both shifters," Luna says, motioning to her and Alice as we climb down the stairs. "And it was still terrifying to walk through the doors of the Tremblay estate. Considering where we come from."

"They've only been welcoming to us," Luna says. "Despite our pasts, where we come from. None of that matters."

We're all heading down to the cellar because though none of the Tremblays are witches or warlocks, they've apparently got a nice stock of spell supplies down there for projects they've hired witches to do for them. Mrs. Tremblay tells me that wards have definitely been cast before, just not for a few years. I'm hoping that means they'll already have all the supplies I'll need though if not, I'll just make a run to the magic shop in town.

I get to know the mates while we're gathering the supplies together. Nothing is organized in the cellar of the Tremblay estate. There's a lot of dusty old furniture and a lot of boxes and a ton of wine. The wine is organized, but not the magic supplies which are scattered around a few different shelves in a dark corner. The place is so stately and grand, I can't help but be a little surprised by how...normal the cellar is. It's almost like anyone else's fancy cellar except for how big and old the furniture is and how much expensive wine is sitting around on shelves.

I reference all the ingredients I'll need for my ward brews. I've got everything on an iPad and I scroll down the list as Michelle and Luna and Alice blow the dust off boxes and unpack jars and vials.

Suddenly Michelle gasps and we all come running over in the dim light of the low ceilinged basement. "What's the matter?" I say.

"Pictures," Michelle says softly. She's opened a shoe box and we all crowd to see a messy pile of photographs of the boys as kids. In some of them, a couple of the boys are shifted while the other ones are human.

"Oh my God, Xander..." Michelle holds up a picture of

Xander hugging a small gray wolf as little Aaron and Micah are sprawled on the grass, wrestling and laughing. "And the wolf must be Mason?"

"Yeah," Alice says fondly. "That's his coloring."

We let ourselves waste just a few minutes looking at the old pictures and then we hunker down and get back to work. But I see Alice smiling to herself as she carefully sets the shoebox aside so we can easily find it later. We dig out all the ingredients and then we get to brewing. None of the other women are witches or anything but they don't need to be. The brew just needs my magic to work and their chanting will amplify the power of the wards if they help me out.

Mrs. Tremblay seems fascinated by it as all as I make up the brew in the kitchen. It's got a seemingly endless list of ingredients, some of which need to be prepared themselves first. Then there's the brew and then we have to circle the *entire* estate, spilling the brew here and there as we chant. Then there's a separate brew for the interior and a different one for the forest. The forest we're doing last after we patrol it and clean it up a bit so that interlopers can't so easily find places to hide. Mrs. Tremblay puts the entire estate staff on the job. That's after she gives them the score; the Tremblays are at war. She asks them if they want to fight, it's not a demand. She assures them they can all go home until it's over and no one would think less of them. But of course, in the end, they all stay. I think it attests to the loyalty the Tremblays tend to inspire.

Everyone's moved into the estate now. That was Xander's mandate though I think everyone feels safer here together. The luxury of the place *is* overwhelming. I haven't had much chance to enjoy it with everything going on but it's hardly what I'm used to. My father's place was nice but most of the time I was in a little bedroom built off his lab. I sometimes went into the main house but not as often as a regular kid

149

would. And after that, I was a scrappy little urchin, trying to get by before the coven took me. I've never even seen a place like the Tremblay estate. I certainly never imagined I'd be hooked up with the place's heir and helping strategize its defence in a war.

Life is...weird.

~

Everything feels very rushed for a couple of days. We don't know when Didion and his people will strike and we still don't know where they are though Xander has put out feelers. That's before he goes to the board meeting with Mason and announces that he's handing over the reigns as CEO to his brother. I had a queasy feeling about that but then I've been at the company for such a short time. From all the research I initially did on the company, I knew Mason had good relationships there. But I'm still a little surprised at the response. People take it very well. Xander tells them he's "exploring new opportunities" and taking a break from such heavy executive responsibilities. Everyone seems pretty understanding though I suppose they're looking at it as the calm after a storm. But his stock price evened out and the shareholders seem much less panicked so that's good.

Mason gives a nice speech and when asked if anything has changed on the suspension of the Godrun drone, he very diplomatically says that he will respect the last decision that his brother made for the company. Then he starts talking about the conversation between the company and Chile and the cleaning up of the mines. Then everybody toasts. I can't believe how relieved Xander seems afterwards. I'm glad for him. That means it was the right decision. If it wasn't, I know he'd be even more on edge.

The evening after the board meeting, when we return to the estate, is not so happy.

There's a message waiting for us at the front gates of the estate.

It's a wolf's head nailed to the stone pillar on one side of the iron gates in front of the mansion. I don't see it at first. I'm texting Alice on my phone as we all drive back in Mason's car and then I hear Xander hiss and mutter curses under his breath. He practically leaps from the car, almost before Mason comes to a stop.

"Shit," is all Mason says.

We all get out and that's when I see it; a big brown wolf's head all gory and bloody and hanging by a rope nailed right into the stone, making an angry hole. The wolf's head hangs open, its tongue lolling out.

Mason says, "That's...that's...blasphemous."

"But they're wolves too," I say, feeling confused as to the message of the whole thing.

"Exactly," Xander says darkly. "You never kill your own kind of species as a shifter. To do so sends the strongest kind of message. It's supposed to be blasphemous." He grimaces as he reaches up to unhook the rope and I see the disturbed expression on his face as he carries the wolf's head through the now open gates through which I see an ocean of unfamiliar cars parked. "Looks like we got our soldiers!" Xander says over his shoulder. "Park the car, Mason. It's time to bunker down."

∽

There's a balcony on the east side of the Tremblay mansion. There are actually five balconies but this one faces east. Xander and his father says when they come, they'll come from the east and from the woods. The estate is crowded

151

now. And there are shifters *everywhere* outside, mainly out front and out in the woods here and there beyond it. It's a good thing the estate is pretty far from any neighbors because the place is lousy with wolves.

Inside, things feel pretty tense. Took us another day to get completely ready and after that it was just waiting but there has been a feeling all day as if *they* are coming. They meaning, my father for one. I'm hoping I don't actually see him.

When Xander insisted I go with Mrs. Tremblay, Michelle and Trevor to a *hidden* room underneath the wine cellar where we would be safest, I didn't want to agree to it. Just because I couldn't shift, didn't mean I couldn't fight. I was actually a little bit offended. I'm a witch after all. I was thinking I could brew up some hexes to have at the ready if anyone came at me if nothing else. But then I see the look in Xander's eyes when he pleads with me. It's a shifter thing and it might be an alpha thing. Alice and Luna can shift. Xander's mom, Michelle, and I cannot. That doesn't mean it's our war, but it does mean that Xander and Aaron and Xander's father would drive themselves nearly mad with worry if we were out there. There was already a little scuffle between Alice and Luna and their boys. Micah and Mason tried to stop them from joining the fight. But they didn't have a single wolf leg to stand on on that front. Not with two women raised in the Hardwidge pack. From what I've heard so far, they can be pretty brutal when they want to be.

"You feel helpless," Mrs. Tremblay says to Michelle and I. Michelle's got Trevor in her arms and he's fast asleep. They've made the hidden room in the cellar comfy for us with a couch and plenty of supplies. There's even cable TV. Not that we're watching. There is, blessedly, cell reception and Wi-Fi. "I know how you feel. I know it well. But you're not."

"Sure feels like it," I say under my breath, but I smile at

Mrs. Tremblay to let her know I'm not angry. I'm just not used to ever being side-lined from a fight. I'm a witch and I'm an activist. I jump in and act whenever I feel like a fight needs to be had. It was only the assurance that Xander would be distracted if he thought I was in danger that's keeping me down here.

"Now how are you two helpless?" Mrs. Tremblay says, laughing. She's sitting in an easy chair behind the sofa. She turns the TV on but leaves it on mute, absently flipping around. "You too did the bulk of securing this place. I fed everyone. They'd be lost without us."

That makes me smile to myself. I do think Xander would be a little lost without me. Or anyway, he might still be at home with his panic and a bottle of whiskey if I hadn't given him a pep talk and bolstered him. I love how well we understand each other.

I tilt my head and squint at Mrs. Tremblay who seems absurdly calm as she rocks forward and back a little in her chair. "Do you...really not mind that I'm human, Mrs. Tremblay? And you don't think Mr. Tremblay minds?"

"Oh..." She waves a hand, dismissing the very subject "That was always going to happen someday. Michelle and I are humans too. You can say we have a shifter gene but your father was a shifter, wasn't he? Hell, you're more shifter than we are. And those rules needed to be changed a long time ago. You and Xander are right. Times are changing. Just...have to fight this war first."

"Yeah." I swallow and fold my hands in my lap. All we can do now is wait. But I have a feeling, I just have a feeling, that the fight is on its way. "All we can do is wait."

CHAPTER SIXTEEN: XANDER

"They're coming," my father says.

We've been waiting for two days. I *hate* waiting. I feel like I'm doing nothing.

I know that I'm not. When Micah and Mason went out to round up our allies, he found out that a few stalwart friends infiltrated Didion's men and are sabotaging wherever they can, mainly in regards to weaponry. That explosive that blew up Aaron's car still haunts me. It's the most unshifter-like behavior I can think of from a group that's supposedly are all about preserving the most traditionally shifter way of life possible.

Bunch of hypocrites.

We've heard varying estimates as to how many wolves Didion's got. I've heard anything from one hundred to a thousand. Well, I've got about five hundred people in total defending the estate and thereby defending the entire clan.

So...it's hard to tell how this is going to go down.

"I don't smell anything," I say to my father.

We're standing on the east wing balcony. I can see a few stretches of road beyond the estate and I can make out a few of our wolves; little dots trotting back and forth, on patrol and on the lookout for any of Didion's men.

"I can smell them," my father says slowly, and just as a breeze sends the scent upwind, I catch it. My jaw tightens and I catch the scent of a whole bunch of shifters that aren't us. I don't know everyone's scent by heart but this is definitely something different. It's faintly metallic, which is odd. And just like we surmised, it's coming from the east. That's good.

I distributed walkie-talkies around to some of the men who can then signal wolves.

"Micah, they're coming from the east," I say into the walkie-talkie. "Get ready."

The attack, when it finally comes, is both sloppy and brutal. There are more wolves on their side than I'd thought there would be. I really didn't think Didion would find many allies and I suspect he's brought up some people from Oregon to join him. They've got numbers. The horde of wolves is visible not just from the east but from the woods. They just keep *coming* just as we knew they would.

It's dispiriting to me, how many shifters Didion and the Hardwidge men were able to convince to join them. Then again, I'm sure he gave them the hard sell on their joined philosophy of bringing back the old ways of shifters, saving the future. Through brutality that is.

I take a deep breath and watch the wolves come streaming down the road toward the estate. Already our wolves on patrol are coming up against them. I watch two of Didion's clash with one of ours and then go rolling out of sight into the woods.

"Okay," I mutter, stepping back inside. "Let's get down there."

Downstairs, the place is packed but now we all head outside, mostly toward the woods though I make sure to have men around the front gates. All but a skeleton crew of those who would remain human, hiding around to keep watch and communicate as needed, are shifted. I head out to the back and shift, trotting down to stand in front of my father and my brothers near the rose garden. It's getting on toward evening now. Mason came home as soon as he could get away and I'm grateful. Not that I love putting anymore of my family than necessary in harm's way.

I can hear them all coming; us and them. I feel a keen sense of territoriality. They're coming to destroy my family and my home. This is the place I played as a child and learned to lead.

They won't take it from us.

I throw my head back and howl and my father and brothers join me. And then I hear the rest of our men out there, the ones who aren't already engaged in battle, howling along with us. I feel a strength coursing through me and I don't feel panicky at all. When the howl fades I crouch, ready to attack and when the first of the Hardwidge wolves come pouring out of the forest with their teeth bared, I do not hesitate.

We ate a lot of meat before the battle to strengthen us and I feel as if my blood is alive and electric. The thing is, I like the fight. I don't enjoy hurting anyone but there is a rush to it. It's not something I'm particularly proud of, it doesn't seem like something a person *should* be proud of but I find myself growling like a mad wolf as I leap forward and catch the oncoming enemy by his throat and we go tumbling hard to the ground.

Wolf shifter combat is notoriously brutal. We go at it with

tooth and claw and the fights are ugly and fast. Unless two wolves are perfectly matched, one usually wins out or gets away and retreats pretty quickly. I also certainly don't enjoy killing other wolves at all but that's the only option now as my paws pound the grass and then the mud of the woods as we begin to push the enemy right back. My teeth sink into the grimy fur of throat after throat and flank after flank.

I go at it in the woods for a while and we seem to be pushing them back rather well and then I see my own people running east which probably means somebody somewhere has been signalled and I follow.

Didion's men are coming around the front so I head back through the woods and I'm let back in through the house to go to the front. No one has breached the line of the woods. It only occurs to me now that Olivia's wards are holding well. They haven't broken through them although I suspect they'll try. It's almost amusing to watch them be physically repelled. They've broken up the gates but an invisible force is holding them back as I watch from a window inside. They run back again, seemingly to regroup and I shift back just as my dad, in human form, comes running in from the back.

"The wards are holding," I tell him. "I can't tell if they have a warlock or anything out there or not..."

My blood feels hot, almost as if it's too hot for my body. If Didion is out there at the gates and I take him down...the battle would be half over. If we can figure the warlock or witch who might be trying to break the wards and take him out before he breaks them, it would be probably three quarters over.

My dad is standing there in his opulent foyer with a ripped up and bloody shirt. His human hands are scuffed and bloody and his limp looks worse when he walks up to me, his mouth caked and gory with blood.

He's short of breath when he says, "You look like you're

waiting for permission to go out there and finish this," he says, panting. "Don't wait. You and me, son. Let's go."

"Hey!" Aaron appears behind us. We all look pretty messed up and gross and pretty much like serial killers but to my surprise Micah looks the worst even as he flexes and fixes me with a steady glare, his sandy blonde hair slicked with blood and dirt.

"Not without us, you don't," Micah says, all but licking his chops. Sometimes I forgot what he went through at that Hardwidge compound. Before that, I didn't even know how strong he was.

We all nod at each other and then I throw open the front door of the estate and we shift. They smell us coming but there's not much they can do. To our surprise and delight, we find Jack Didion and a shifter I recognize as the lackey to Alice's brother. I heard a rumor he was Jack's lieutenant. Looks like the rumor was true. Sure enough, down the road I spy a human who I can tell from here, doesn't smell like a shifter. He's trying to stay out of the way but he's holding a candle and his eyes are fixed on the house as he mutters to himself, two other younger men standing with him and chanting along.

A warlock.

I glance at Micah as we run down the drive to the open gates, on the attack. I try to nod in the direction of the warlock, hoping he'll get me and he gives me a nod.

I wouldn't want to be that warlock right now.

Meanwhile, there's Didion and his men, all in wolf form now as they rear back, bearing their teeth and refusing to run as we pound through the gates. Didion and I run straight for each other.

I've never wanted to kill anyone more in my life.

I can't get to his throat because he mashes his head against mine so that we see stars and then we roll into the dirt, scrambling to find purchase and I roll us so I'm on top of him, kicking with my legs. He's good at dodging and he's fast but I can feel his age. He's not going to last.

I go for the kill repeatedly and he manages to dodge but that's okay. I can wear him out.

I don't know what's going on around me. There is only Didion and I at each other's throats, every muscle in me tense, my focus a laser that is centered only on defeating Didion and preferably not ending his life. The only reason I would is so that we can question him and find out if he has any men hiding out there with some kind of back-up plan for his defeat.

But I'd still rather kill him.

His claws are long and sharp. They're not the dulled claws of older alphas. I feel like they've been enhanced somehow, perhaps with magic. I shimmy and shift even as I catch his shoulders in my jaws and bite down as hard as I can manage, feeling him quake with pain. It makes me want to hurt him more, to hurt him as much as he hurt Olivia and tried to hurt Michelle. With a twist of our bodies, it all happens quite suddenly. I catch the soft tissue of his belly in my mouth and I rip through it like butter just as I feel the white hot pain of his claws ripping through my shoulder. It hurts like hell, his claws make a tear from the top of my shoulder down the center of my chest and it's bloody as hell but it's not too deep.

I won't die.

But he will.

It's over abruptly. I'm biting through stomach, through organs, his blood hot in my mouth and I can feel him slowing, his weight suddenly heavy when I roll us and he's half on top of me. Then all at once he's perfectly still and I reflexively scramble to get out from under him only to jump back and get my bearings for a split second to find the next fight.

Except there isn't one.

Not here anyway.

There's only my father and my brothers left now, and a couple of wolf corpses here on the road. I shift back and run to Micah, who's standing there in the road, catching his breath, staring at the dead warlock.

"Micah!" I shout, and a sharp stab of pain blooms in my shoulder as the shock of my injury wears off. I'm bleeding pretty badly but it's not a gusher anyway. "Where are the other two?"

"Took off," he says, wiping his bloody mouth before he spits into the street. "They were just paid to help the wizard here. He's dead. Didion?"

"Dead," I say, looking around for my dad who I could swear was just standing here.

Now he's sitting in the road looking pale with pain as Aaron runs over to him.

"Dad?" I say, kneeling beside him.

"I'm fine, just hurt my leg a little." He sees my shoulder and grimaces. "You need that wrapped up."

"But..." I shake my head, still panting. They'll never break the wards and get in now, not with the warlock dead and with their leader gone too, the rest will probably flee or surrender. But I need to see that happen before I can rest. "The woods..."

"You're gonna bleed out, dumbass," Micah says, rubbing my back. "Get inside. We've all but won."

It's the "but" that worries me but they won't leave me alone until I go in and head to the kitchen where a few shifters are waiting with medical supplies for the wounded. Marie Vallen is the alpha's wife from Tacoma and when she sees my shoulder, she glares at me like I've done something wrong.

"You sit down right now," she snaps. I sit at a stool at the

160

counter. It's quiet in here. Weirdly quiet considering there's still chaos going on outside. But the wards Olivia cast are too strong. Nobody's getting inside. We're safe. My mate is safe. And Jack Didion is dead.

A couple hours later, the last of the enemy has surrendered.

～

"Baby, your shoulder!" Olivia says, appearing in the doorway of the study.

I've been waiting for Olivia to appear from out of the basement for what seems like hours because my mother won't let me move from my seat in the study due to my injury. The place is still full of our people and there's a hubbub of people being stitched up and looked after.

There are some casualties, of course. I'm thankful it's nobody from my family but when guilt starts creeping up on me somebody from my clan will walk up and shake my hand even as I'm bleeding. Calling upon people to fight for you and then seeing some of them lost is not something I've quite experienced before. There was the raid on the Hardwidge compound, of course. But nobody died.

We are helped though by shifter stamina and strength. In the end, we've lost twelve people. Obviously, I'll be providing for their families after this. It's my responsibility and will hardly make a dent in the Tremblay piggy bank.

Olivia grabs a chair and sits beside me looking more worried than I think my injury warrants. Considering my ability to heal quickly, I don't think it will even slow me down for more than a day.

"I'm fine, sweetheart," I say, leaning over to kiss her hair. "I'll be just fine."

She takes a deep breath and nods. "Aaron says you killed him."

I can't read her tone but she doesn't look very upset. "I...Yeah. I had to."

"I'm glad you did," she says softly. "I mean I'm not happy you had to do it or anything... I'm just glad I don't have to worry about him ever again."

I understand what she means. I can't imagine the complicated feelings she must be having over the whole thing. "We captured everyone," I tell her. "No escapees this time. But I don't know if we can keep them all prisoner. Not all of them. I think we might have to...change some hearts and minds on this one."

"I trust your judgement," she says, smiling fondly.

"Me too," I say, sighing. "My judgement was to take your advice and let people help me."

"See? Excellent judgement. So we won the war." Olivia scoots up a little closer and wraps her arms around my neck. "What next, my big alpha mate?"

"Now...the future."

EPILOGUE

Six months later...

"To our mates!" Xander says and the girls and I giggle as our guys get to their feet, all four Tremblay brothers all in a row on the other side of the dining room table. They hold their champagne glasses up.

Everyone's wearing tuxes tonight. It's just a regular full moon tonight and it was Micah who got it in his head to make it a formal event in celebration of the new pack laws that Alice has gotten passed by the clan by an overwhelming vote.

The clan looks a lot different than it used to since, what most shifters in Washington call, the Battle of Tremblay Manor.

There seems to be a new understanding that things have changed. Interacting with humans is something to be careful of but I don't think it's going to have the stigma it used to. I imagine there are going to be more human mates. I'm imagining the "fates" or whatever force it is that pairs shifters with their mates for life is actually trying to save the shifters.

My theory is that by evolutionary necessity, humans will be able to have shifter children.

At least...that's what I'm hoping.

"To our mates!" All the brothers say.

Everyone takes a sip of their champagne...except me. I actually pretend to sip it but not a drop slips past my lips. I glance around to see if anyone has noticed and immediately Xander squints at me across the table. I wasn't going to tell him yet. I was going to save it for when we were alone. I've only had the news a day.

Michelle once told me that when she was pregnant, Aaron could smell it on her. I wonder if Xander hasn't yet because I'm fully human? Whatever the reason, I'm happy to surprise.

Except the way his eyes are widening as he looks at me pointedly not drinking my champagne, I think that surprise is spoiled now.

"I think Tremblay Company deserves a toast to!" I say, getting to my feet and weakly attempting to distract Xander.

"Hell yeah, it does," Xander says, raising his glass. "Stock's just broken a record after the Ethical Works Initiative."

Mason looks a little sheepish and he waves a hand as if attempting to dismiss both of us. "That was as much Olivia's idea as mine-"

"Yeah well, good job listening to Olivia," Xander says, winking at Mason. "God knows, it's the smartest thing I've ever done."

After a typically boisterous dinner that goes late until the boys along with Luna and Alice are starting to get edgy to go shift, the couples pair up and go for a little walk as the moon rises.

Xander wraps an arm around my waist as we make our way out to the breezy evening. He's leading me in the direction of the rose garden but that seems to be where everyone else wants to go to.

"Used to be," Xander says, "that the rose garden wasn't packed with canoodling Tremblays every full moon. And now look at us?"

I spy Micah and Luna giggling and running off to go make out behind a particularly tall hedge and it makes me chuckle. "Well, it is very romantic. Maybe you guys could put in another garden? Plant some begonias or something."

"Oh yeah," Xander says wryly. "Nothing more romantic than begonias."

The way he says that makes me laugh and we stand there, facing each other and I watch the way he looks at me like he can't imagine being with anyone else. He twirls a lock of my hair around his finger before kissing me softly.

"I saw you at dinner," he says, laying soft little kisses to my cheek and my jaw and making his way down to my neck. "You don't like champagne suddenly?"

"I don't know what you're talking about," I say, wrapping my arms around his waist.

He leans back and smiles slyly. "Is there something I should know?"

"Oh, Xander Tremblay, I'm guessing there are about a thousand things you should know," I say, laughing.

"Maybe if I tell you something you'll tell me something," Xander murmurs into my throat. "How about that?"

"You can try." I grin and pull him tight against me. I love this flirty Xander. It's become one of my three favorite versions of Xander.

"Okay. How about this... I bought your old apartment building in Lynwood." He leans back and smiles, smug as anything and I squint at him, genuinely confused.

"Why would you do that?"

"Uh, because you talk about that place all the time and

how run down it is?" Xander says. "I'm gonna fix it up nice. I'm not raising rent or anything like that. Those kids you still sell the potions to need a nice place to live, don't they? I mean it's nice they got the outreach program you started over there but an elevator in that place would be helpful. Some new coats of paint, working heat..." I'm staring at him, moony-eyed and he grins. "You like that?"

"I *love* that," I say, squeezing him tight and leaning against him. "I love that you did that."

"Now you tell me somethin'," he murmurs in my ear.

"What could I possibly tell you?" I say, biting my lip and enjoying this playfulness.

"Oh, I don't know. Maybe that you're got a little baby Tremblay in there?" He pats my stomach and I smile against this lips.

"Oh yeah, that."

"Hey, I want you to know something," Xander says now, leaning back. He cups my cheek and kisses the tip of my nose. "Shifter or human...doesn't matter to me. It really doesn't. I love you. I love this kid no matter what. Love them already."

"Aww, you're already a good daddy," I say, kissing his cheek.

"I'm so happy," he whispers in my ear. "Can't even tell you."

"I know." I grin up at him. "We can tell everybody in a while. Let's just sit with it right now."

"Definitely. And now the good daddy needs to go get his wolf out," Xander says, kissing my mouth one more time. "I'm all giddy and he's pawing at the door."

I smack his shoulder. "Go get em'!" He backs away from me, seeming reluctant but I can already see Micah and Mason trotting off to the woods. "I'll hang out with mom and Michelle!"

He blows a kiss and I roll my eyes but I blow one back. I jog out to watch him shift before he runs into the woods. It's my favorite part of these dinners. Sometimes I wish I could share the run with him and know what it's like to be a wolf. But we have our own runs when he curls up next to me under a tree and we just sit for a while, comfortable in each other's presence.

Now I watch my alpha trot off with his brothers and Luna and Alice and I think to myself: *My brothers, my sisters...*

Because human as I am, I'm still one of the pack now and I have a family now that's better than any family I would have wished for.

Because nothing says love and family like the Tremblay pack.

AFTERWORD

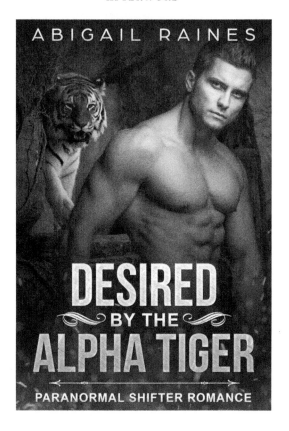

Click The Link Below To Get Desired By The Alpha Tiger
https://mailchi.mp/3f079082ad5b/abi

Hope you truly enjoyed the book! If you didn't like the book, please let me know why and what I can do to make it a better experience for you.

Interested in more from Abigail Raines? Check out my Amazon page for more and follow me!

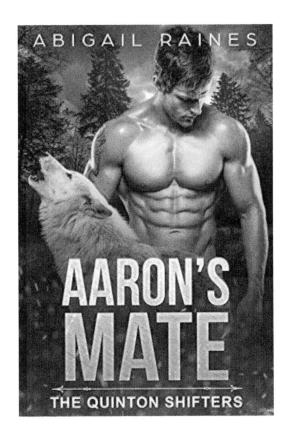

Check out Aaron's Mate, the first book of the Quinton Shifters
Series.

Aaron always followed pack rules...until he didn't.

Rule#1: Fealty to pack
 Rule #2: Loyalty to clan
 Rule#3: Avoid humans

Aaron spent years resisting the charms of the human woman,

Michelle.

Then, resisting her became impossible.

But...

Shifters don't fall in love with humans.

And...

Shifters can't get humans pregnant.

When a night of shared passion proves both these to be fallacies, Aaron has a new problem on his hands.

To keep her, he must challenge his pack, his clan, his alpha and centuries of tradition.

He'll fight to the death to protect both his child and his woman, But can their love survive with all odds stacked against them?

Warning: Intended for mature adults 18 and over!

Read Now!

ABOUT THE AUTHOR

Abigail is a very romantic and open minded lady. She writes mainly Paranormal Shifter Romance and Contemporary Romance. She loves spending time with her 2 finicky cats, her 2 shy dogs (they are twin sisters) and her husband. She lives in Lewisville, Texas and LOVES it there!

Check out other books in the series by clicking on the covers.

Website
Facebook